Dukedom Rumble

A Chase to Remember

Eric Kercher

Paper and Sword, LLC

For all those that encourage, uplift, and inspired me and others to dream. They gave me hope for the future and meaning of a life dedicated to the Lord.

From the Author

There are days when we all need an escape from a terrible job, a terrible day, or a terrible life.

Join my newsletter and get an escape from the real world, stories, and lore designed to entertain and delight.

You'll also get *Stories from the Deep*, an exclusive, unpublished anthology chock full of extra epilogues, short stories, and lore from the Patmos Sea Fantasy Adventure Series.

Join now at erickercher.com.

Enjoy the book.

-Eric Kercher

Chapter One

Scott was getting ready for a date that would never happen. By the time he shaved and showered, the humid bathroom air thick with the smell of peppermint shaving cream, he had expected her to have called, and he checked his phone.

Just an empty, blue screen. No missed calls. He tossed the phone back onto his bed and ignored the worry that was building.

He dressed quickly, throwing on a nice, if not a bit wrinkled, shirt and some slacks. They were comfortable and eased onto his clean skin. She still had not called that night, out of character for Brianna. So Scott began to ask around. He called Becky who picked up on the second ring.

"Yeah, she was here this morning picking up her book from a few nights ago. She had left it here and went home for the night," Becky said. "But she hasn't called me for anything else, is she okay?" Scott could hear the fear creeping into her voice.

"I'm not sure, but she's probably fine," Scott said, but knew in his heart it wasn't true. The feeling was deep inside him, in the pit of his stomach like a cold bullet lodged in his gut. His cold apartment mocked him, making it worse. After he hung up the phone with Becky he knew he had to go to her house.

He got in his car and began the familiar drive to her place. She valued her privacy very highly and had elected to go with a small, but still pricey, efficiency apartment with no roommates. Scott cursed under his breath, hoping that she would be there. She lived downtown, above one of the coffee shops that used to be a house but had been converted a decade or two prior. One of those grand, stately homes that the owners had fallen down on their luck and needed to vacate. The upstairs had been converted to multiple apartments to make money. She loved the smell of coffee that wafted up to her room every morning, slowly waking her up.

He parked in the street behind it and quickly bounded up the stairs to the landing. Her door was the far right in a set of three and he knocked on it loudly. Even this late, she would have been up studying. There was no response. Scott crept up on the roof using the shortcut he had discovered a few months back and climbed the ledge to her bedroom window. It was dark inside. He paused. His breath was quick. His heart beat quicker. He grabbed the handle and pulled. He slipped inside.

There was no one in the room. The kitchen, really a small kitchenette consisting of a stove, refrigerator, and sink with a few cabinets was crushed up against the far wall with the entrance door. The bed was next to the window with a small table in between. The only other room was the bathroom, a cramped room barely bigger than the stand-up shower and toilet that were flanking a small sink. The door was shut so Scott made his way over to it, but he knew before he opened it that it was empty. Houses have a certain feel if they are occupied, a warmth as if they are happy that someone was living in them, but there was no warmth here. Just the cold, empty feel of the dark. He opened the door and saw his silhouette in the mirror, the only living being in the apartment.

Scott slumped down, his back coming to rest on the footboard of the bed. He sat in the dark for a few minutes, thinking—and feeling the cold feeling in the pit of his stomach grow larger. She was not here, but she should have been. Where was she? Did he do something that had made her angry? They fought occasionally, but not any more than the usual couple.

His mind immediately went to the worst. Something bad had happened. He reached into his backpack and pulled out his laptop, activating it. He pulled up the synchronization function and began to run it. He had tried calling her on her phone, but she didn't pick up. She had authorized him to track her phone so he entered his pass key and selected her phone. An error message flashed on the projection screen in front of him, casting a red glow around the room. Unable to detect location kept flashing, suspended in midair. He tossed the laptop on the bed and got up, going to turn on the lights.

He froze as soon as he turned them on. The front door had looked fine from the outside, but from inside with the lights on he saw that there was some form of forced entry. The jamb had cracked around the door handle as if someone had wanted to get in in a hurry. Scott looked more closely around the room, this time noticing small details that stood out as bright as day. Small things were out of place, like the chairs and some utensils on the small amount of counter space available. It was as if whoever had come into the apartment had put everything back but didn't know her well enough to know that she was very particular about where it went.

Now that Scott knew, the cold feeling in his stomach turned hot with rage. He felt it in his body as it worked its way to his ears. And he knew he was angry when his ears became hot. He turned back to the laptop, picking it up and taking a three-dimensional scan of the room. He pulled out one of the two chairs in the room and got to work.

He pulled up the synchronization function and targeted her secret phone, the one they had decided on years ago. This wasn't a pretty town, it had a seedy underbelly that was bigger than the good parts. Focusing in he found a location that popped up. Setting the triangulation function took time so Scott prowled the room, looking for more cues using his laptop camera filter functions.

The ground had been sterilized, with no footprints showing up in any electromagnetic spectrum, not in infrared or ultraviolet. Whoever had done this was a professional, which worried Scott. Her laptop was missing, which wasn't surprising considering the amount of information on it. Whoever had broken into her apartment would likely have taken it. A small chime sounded, and Scott pulled the sync function back up.

He became puzzled. The last location that he could triangulate from the data was far away, but not anywhere she would normally go. *Why would she be out there?* he thought to himself. It only took a few seconds for it to click when he realized she had been kidnapped. Someone had taken her against her will. He sat back in the chair, stunned at the realization. It made sense, the entry, the odd location, someone cleaning up the apartment.

Emotions raged within Scott, pulling him in every direction. He was angry and afraid, full of hate and despair, torn between action and inaction. If he had only been there when it had happened things might have been different. He sat there for a few minutes eating himself away inside until he was disturbed by the soft alert of his cell phone. He pulled himself together and answered it in audio mode, not wanting to let Rob know where he was right away.

"Hey, man," Scott said.

"Hey, where are you?" Rob sounded a little bit annoyed. Scott realized how late it was and that he had missed his meeting with Rob by a half hour already. "Yo, Scott, are you there?" Scott had not said anything to Rob and cleared his throat, steeling himself.

"...I'd rather not talk right now. Something's come up." Even though they were extremely close he still hesitated telling him. "Actually, something has happened. Can you meet me at my place?" There was a slight pause as Rob digested his words.

"What's happened, Scott?" he said softly.

"I'll tell you when you get there," Scott replied.

"Okay, I'll be right over." Rob hung up. Scott wasn't sure if the same people who took her would be able to track him or Rob but he wasn't willing to take that chance. He had to assume they were aware of who he was and that they were against him. There was no way this was not premeditate, someone had deliberately broken into the apartment and tried to clean up after themselves. She knew how to handle herself too, she wouldn't have been caught off guard easily and would have resisted. They had to have been professionals. Scott scanned the room one last time before packing up his laptop into his backpack.

He saw the picture of them on the nightstand, her favorite one. They were up in the mountains for a long weekend, hiking out off the grid. The memory of it flashed back into his mind as he stood there. Her beautiful hair shimmering in the sunlight swaying in the light breeze as they stumbled upon the meadow filled with flowers. The smell was incredible, as if the flowers themselves were trying to make the bees buzzing around them drunk with the sweetness. They stopped and watched the sunset, the entire valley spread out before them, an evening mist creeping up from the river. She took the picture then, as they were arrayed in flowers in the brilliant golds and reds of the sunset.

"For when my nights get cold," she had said. "Then I can remind myself of the warmth of this night and the warmth in my heart." A wave of sadness washed through Scott, rocking the very depths of who he was. He could picture himself in that meadow with her, feel the cool breeze and the warmth of her hand.

"Find me," he could hear her say. His hand clenched as his resolve strengthened. Scott left the same way he came, as familiar to him as the back of his hand. He climbed out the window and across the roof to the landing, feeling cold inside.

It took him a few minutes to make his way back to his place. They had chosen to live close enough to each other to make the trip short but not too close to tempt them to always be with each other. As he hopped into his car he pulled out his laptop and connected it to the net-sphere within it, activating the autopilot to take him there. His car was old enough to have a manual override, unlike the newer models that were completely self-driving. Scott occasionally liked to take the wheel and feel the power of the engine if the mood struck him. But tonight he needed to focus all of his energy on her.

He pulled up the scan he had taken and began to search for clues. He had a diagnostic program running in the background to flag anything he had missed. It was still running when he made it back and paused it to move inside. His apartment was old enough to not be wired, but he still maintained a small net-sphere to run his laptop and a few other electronics like the imager he threw his scan up on. The diagnostic had noted the broken door and the leaky faucet in the kitchen, one the landlord refused to fix even though she had complained enough, and had come up with one more hit that he hadn't noticed before.

There, in the corner of the room, was something that had been left there very intentionally. A small recording device was hidden in her room designed to look like a screw on the nightstand leg. It had flashed on its small magnetic field put out by the tiny amount of current flowing through the electronics. Scott didn't remember her putting anything like that in her apartment by herself but he couldn't have been sure it wasn't hers. The nightstand was fairly recent, she had picked it up at one of her favorite stores which happened to be a thrift store. But she had bought it a few months ago, it had matched her style exactly, as if someone had made it just for her. He was still looking over the results when he heard the door chime and the security camera display pop up into the foreground of the imager.

Rob stood outside, clearly agitated. Scott went over to the door and let him in.

"What's going on Scott?" Rob asked again, more insistent than when he was on the phone. Scott motioned him in and headed back to the imager.

"It's probably nothing," he said. A thought occurred to him that if they were able to get to her then they might have bugged his place. He flipped up his diagnostic and began to run it on his apartment. "I just have to check something out." Scott gestured toward the imager and Rob glanced at it. His eyes widened a small amount, revealing some surprise but hidden to almost all except his best friend. Scott knew that he was surprised if he revealed even that much.

"OK..." Rob said, sitting down on the couch and waiting for the diagnostic to conclude. They sat in silence for a while, since it took a lot to compute through that much data, even for his optical net-sphere. Rob looked a little uneasy as he ran his fingers through his hair, pulled his laptop out and spun it around his knuckles. He had learned to do that in the third grade and anytime he had to wait he would always do it. Scott sat in the silence, retreating into his own thoughts. The world was bad, true, but this really didn't make sense. What kind of evil would be willing to take her?

Based on the evidence that he had this had to be premeditated somehow. The planning was too good, the cleanup too precise. It had to be sophisticated enough to be someone with resources to be able to pull it off, which meant that most of the young gangs were out, and they had to evade a lot of security. Her apartment was gated in the back, and the front lay on a well-traveled road, which meant a lot of security out front. A small chime from his imager brought him back into the present, and he stood up to walk over to the display.

The scan had revealed one unknown electronic signature, emanating from his bedroom. Scott motioned to Rob who was watching carefully and Rob joined him at the image. Scott pulled the results onto his laptop, and Rob followed him to the room. Scott followed the electronic signature to a pen located on his desk. He snapped it in half, shattering the body into two large pieces. Some ink splattered onto his hands and the floor where he had ruptured the inkwell. He cursed and wiped his hands on a dirty shirt on the floor, handing the clean side to Rob.

"Well, this is interesting," Rob said. He was peering into the broken end of the pen. Scott continued wiping off his hands and the other side of the pen. Rob dumped the contents of the pen onto the desk. It contained the mechanical device used to retract and project the pen tip, but it also had a small chip device. Rob whipped out his laptop and placed the chip onto the analysis pad, booting up a diagnostic program. Scott peered into the somewhat clean tip of the pen and dumped it out onto the table as well. All he came up with was the broken pen tip and a spring.

"That is not as interesting," Scott replied, in reference to his side of the pen. He stared at the projection from Rob's laptop as the program ran. "Is it dead?" he asked. Rob shot him a look.

"I think you made sure of that," Rob replied sarcastically, pointing to the snapped antenna Scott had not noticed before.

"Nice," Scott said. "Now, who would want to bug little old me?"

"That's a good question," Rob said, "along with where did you get this pen?" Scott picked up the pen and turned it over in his hands. The lettering on the pen was not familiar to him, which wasn't surprising considering how little he used paper. That was always more of her deal. A memory flashed into his head as he thought it.

"I don't think this is mine," Scott replied. "Look, it says Middleton National Contractors. I think she picked this up at a career fair a few months ago or something and left it here." Rob snatched it out of his hands to read it himself.

"Yeah, that does seem a little odd considering you have a job and all. This doesn't look like you picked it up in the hospital waiting room either," Rob said, turning it over in his hands as he waited for the program to finish. "It looks like this is pretty common. I don't think we're going to get far on it," Rob stated, scrolling through the unfinished results. Scott sighed and sat down on the bed.

"That does make more sense if it does belong to her," Scott said.

"How so?" Rob asked.

"Well, that's what I was going to talk to you about. I haven't heard from Briana today. I went over to her apartment this evening and found that it was broken into, but someone had cleaned it up."

"What? What do you mean broken into?" Rob asked incredulously.

"I mean someone had forced their way in through the door and had broken the jamb, but it was hidden from the outside, and they also put everything back into its place to cover it up," Scott replied.

"How do you know they put it back if they cleaned it up?" Rob asked.

"Mainly from the chairs," Scott said.

"Ah," Rob said. That was all Scott needed to say. Briana had a very particular way of wanting things put back and anyone who was familiar enough to go over to her house learned very quickly. Still, she wasn't very trusting so this came as a surprise to Rob.

"That's not all," Scott said. "Follow me." They went back into the living room, and Scott pulled up the room display. "You can see the chairs and some of her utensils not in the right spot, but look at this." He pointed to the nightstand.

"It's bugged. Which would make more sense as to why the pen was bugged too. Did she get them together?" Rob asked.

"I don't know, I can't remember, but she picked up the nightstand a few months ago too. It was like it was made for her. I think they specifically targeted her for some reason," Scott said. Rob sat, pondering what he had just said.

"They had to have some good resources available to be able to pull this one off," Rob said. His laptop chimed now, and he pulled up the results of the scan. "I mean, even though we're talking about fairly common stuff here it doesn't mean it's easy to access. You have to have connections and some money at the very least. Just one of these bugs is probably upward of five grand." Scott nodded, agreeing. Rob continued to scroll through the results, finally giving up when he reached the bottom.

"Not much, again, fairly common stuff here. Whoever planted it didn't leave a trace either, which goes back to the professional theory again," Rob said, putting his laptop away, exasperated. "And I doubt the other one is going to give us much more if we go back and retrieve it." He looked over the scan of her apartment again, comparing the energy signatures. "Anyway, what did the cops say?" he asked. Scott stayed silent. Rob turned slowly, Scott would not look him in the eye. "Scott?" he questioned.

"I didn't tell them," Scott replied quietly, steeling himself for the response he knew was coming.

"What do you mean you didn't tell them? It looks a whole lot like Briana was kidnapped, and you don't want to report it? Are you insane?" Scott could tell Rob was getting worked up as he spoke.

"I just know I can't tell them. It's instinct," Scott said.

"It's instinct? Is it really?" Rob asked, still visibly worked up.

"Yes, you have to trust me on this, Rob," Scott said. Rob had stood up as he spun up and now paused. He took a deep breath and sat down. Scott was somewhat impressed.

"Look, Scott, you have to get over that and learn to get help," Rob said, much more calmly after a few more seconds in quiet. Scott didn't need to know what Rob was talking about, it was unspoken and would remain that way. Rob had learned not to talk about it directly a long time ago after a few clashes and didn't need to learn another lesson in beating his head up against a brick wall.

"My instinct has kept me safe in a very dangerous line of work and I'm not about to stop trusting it. The good news is that I still have a lead," Scott said, pulling up the telemetry data. "And it's only a few hours old, which means I might still be able to catch up to whoever took her—"

"Whoa, wait a second. If you're going to do this, then I'm coming with you," Rob said, cutting him off. "You're not going to pull that lone wolf stuff." Scott considered it for a moment, thinking about arguing but then thought better of it. He was about to answer when Rob stopped him again. "And no, you're not going to agree and then leave me when you can lose me. I'm going to do this. Brianna means a lot to me too." Scott stared at him, surprised at how Rob could know what he was thinking. He was considering the plan to just leave Rob somewhere convenient, maybe make him follow a false trail for clues and then not get back with him.

"What about your job? This might take more than a few hours," Scott asked.

"First of all, it's going to take as long as it takes. Secondly, that job is just a front, and you know it. If I really wanted to get a job there would be hundreds of suitors lining up. Even now I get a few from time to time trying to attract me to the dark side," Rob said, getting up and going over to the kitchen, grabbing a glass from the cabinet and filling it with water. "We need to start now though. It will only get harder the colder the trail goes." He took a sip and then pulled out his laptop, executing a few programs.

"I know where to get some gear," Scott said. Rob shot him a look across the room.

"No way, Scott. You will get in some deep trouble if you do that," Rob said. Scott ignored him as he tapped his cell phone. "Really, you can't do that, man." Scott held up a finger to his lips.

"Already too late," Scott said, mildly pleased with the exasperated look on Rob's face. It was true that he would get into some terribly hot water if he "liberated" a few supplies from work but luckily he had a good working relationship with his boss and was relatively certain he could get some authorization.

"Hello?" a man answered sleepily in audio mode only. Scott glanced up at the clock and realized it was already ten o'clock.

"Dave, it's Scott. Sorry to wake you up, I didn't realize how late it is," Scott started, thrown off of his original train of thought. He looked at Rob, realizing his mistake. Rob snickered softly but loud enough for Scott to hear. "Anyway, I need some help."

A long pause on the other end.

"Hold on," the voice on the other end said. They could hear the rustle of sheets as he got out of bed and the soft padding of footsteps on carpeting. A slight creak as the door opened and closed, and then more footsteps. The projection alert flashed on the screen and Scott selected it. All they could see was a moving shadow in the darkness, and then the shadow clicked a lamp on and was bathed in brightness. Dave did not look terribly pleased to be awake. "I hope this is worth waking me up in the middle of the night, Scott," Dave said. Scott glanced over at Rob, again thrown off from his original goal.

"I...I need to borrow some equipment. Also, I'll be taking some time off," Scott blurted out suddenly, suddenly regretting his decision to wake up his boss to borrow company assets. Dave just stared at him, looking like a stern father.

"And I don't get to know why, I'm assuming?" Dave asked.

"I'd rather not talk about it, especially like this," Scott replied. Dave took off his glasses and sighed, rubbing his temple with his other hand and closing his eyes.

"And will Rob need some equipment as well?" Dave said. Rob and Scott started at his being mentioned. Scott had been sure to set up the projection cameras just to record him and not Rob. Somehow he knew that Rob was with him. Scott sighed and expanded the projection camera to include Rob.

"Good evening, Mr. Devos," Rob said. "How did you know I was here?" he asked.

"I didn't. It was a guess that you just confirmed. Also, you have a bad habit of sharing very specific looks between each other," Dave said, putting his glasses back on. A small smirk appeared on his mouth. Scott was a little relieved and couldn't help smiling. Dave had that way about him, able to disarm a tense situation which was very fortunate in his line of work. The two of them again glanced at each other, sheepish looks on their faces.

"That being said, why should I authorize you company funds for a personal expedition?" Dave asked, his face once again serious. Scott recovered his composure and became serious as well. The moral dilemma running through his brain paralyzed him. Dave was a great boss, always looking out for him and a great mentor. He had taught Scott everything he knew. On more than one occasion he had saved his life, so the bond between them was very strong, although it was still a professional relationship. Dave was like a father to him. It hurt Scott not to tell him everything, but he couldn't be sure the connection was safe and he didn't want to risk anything.

"Because I've lost something," Scott said. Dave cocked his head to the side, a sure sign of surprise to those who knew him well but fairly innocent if you didn't. Again, a long silence rang out over the connection. Scott was surprised to find himself impatient, but then realized that it was because of the time limit on them. The longer they sat here doing nothing, the worse it would be later on. Dave scratched his chin.

"OK, you have what you need, Scott. I trust you," Dave said. Part of it was Scott's track record. He didn't lose things that were important but was always losing things that weren't, and never let it get to him. Even when other people pointed it out Scott would acknowledge it and maybe shrug, but never seemed like he cared. Only certain things in his life were assigned such importance that he would keep track of them. Dave leaned forward, suddenly menacing to Rob. "But if you get in trouble, you'd better call me immediately." Scott nodded, comforted in the knowledge that Dave understood that it was important to him. Even if he didn't know it was Briana that had gone missing, Dave had a strong suspicion it was related to her in some way. It was what he cared about the most.

"Thanks, Dave. I owe you," Scott said. Dave snorted.

"Put it on my tab."

Chapter Two

He suited up, putting on his Strength suit, an advanced suit designed for extra power applications when needed. This was the time, if any, for a little extra firepower. Scott knew he would have to abandon it for stealth, but the removable modular backpack was useful as an extra battery, and, if things got really bad, could turn into a bomb if short-circuited. He grabbed his weapons and prepped for battle.

Scott and Rob hopped into the ATV. Rob snuck a glance at Scott and noted his demeanor. Scott was incredibly tense but calm. It was as if his whole life had led up to this moment, a moment of redemption. Their relationship had never been the fairy-tale–perfect time, but they did get through hard times together.

"Rob," Scott said suddenly after turning on the ignition.

"Yeah, Scott?"

"I don't know what I would do without her," he spoke softly, the trepidation in his voice.

"I know, man, I know," Rob replied. They sat for a few more moments in silence, as if feeding on each other in preparation for what was to come. Scott moved his hands to the steering wheel and activated the ATV's silent mode. They began the journey.

***

It was about an hour to the last signal location they had received from Amy. Scott parked the ATV on the leeward side of a ridge, below the sight line as he had been trained, and disembarked with Rob. They were a few hundred meters from the signal location, but they still crept silently into view. Below them, in the valley, was nothing. A copse of trees fed off a wimpy stream down in the valley. After searching for any heat signatures and determining none, they made their way down the hill as silently as the Strength suits would allow. They came upon signs of a small camp, like whoever took her had rested here.

"Why would they stop?" Rob wondered aloud. Scott looked up into the sky, a familiar look of pondering on his face.

"They could have been tired?" Scott said. But they both knew that was not the case. There was no way they would have been tired after an hour of movement. The tracks of the modified SUV clearly came to a stop with footsteps leading to the trees and back but that made no sense.

"Maybe they had to stop for something?" Rob said, which made more sense to both of them.

"Or maybe they had to stop for someone," Scott said, and they both knew why. "She somehow made them stop. Maybe she said she really needed to use the bathroom or something like that. She was fighting, she must have done this on purpose." Rob nodded, and they both began to look for clues. The tracks led to the trees, it looked like two large men based on the footprints. Every once in a while, the steps were marred by odd streaks.

"They were probably carrying her, based on the tracks," Rob said, following them to the trees. They knew they would find something, but it took a while of searching until they did. Scott had branched out after they had searched a thicket where the footsteps had stopped. He had found a branch with leaves covered in blood and needed to cool off when he found it. Hanging off a small plant was her locket. He gingerly picked it up.

"Rob," he said softly, "over here." Very carefully he opened up the locket, seeing his face framed in the heart. Rob made his way over, something in his hands as well.

"I found this." It was her smashed cell phone. Scott's heart dropped.

"That's why we couldn't track her any farther," Scott said.

"I'm surprised they didn't find it sooner," Rob said. Scott shook his head.

"That's because that is her second one she keeps hidden. It was a precaution we took when we were dating to hide it from her parents." Some things clicked in Rob's mind as Scott spoke, remembering actions and memories. Scott began to move with the locket back to the ATV. "Come on, I think that's all we're going to find."

Scott grabbed his pack off the back as soon as they got there and began fumbling through its contents. It was still early in the morning and would be a few hours until dawn so the darkness made it difficult to see. Still, he pulled out his laptop and began to hook up a secret compartment in the locket he opened with a small paper clip. He placed it on the analysis pad of the laptop and entered a few codes to unlock it. Rob stared in amazement—it was somehow a storage device.

"It's like a black box for her. It's set to auto-dump after a week but can record if she activates it with a pass phrase," Scott said as the interface projected into the air. With a few swipes he located the stored audio and activated it. The audio was muffled, as if clothing was rustling against itself. They heard the sound of the car over the microphone, traveling to the place they were now. They could hear what sounded like a male voice, extremely quiet and muffled. They heard the slink of the metal chain—most likely the chain the locket was on—and suddenly the voice was much clearer, although still extremely soft.

"What is he saying?" Rob asked. Scott was intensely watching the projection the audio was creating of the sound waves.

"I'm not sure, I can't make it out," Scott said, exasperated.

"Hold on." Rob pulled out his laptop from his pack and activated it. A thought suddenly struck him. "Hey, do you know why they call these things laptops?"

"I think it's a holdover from the old days, but now is really not the time, Rob," Scott said, still intensely concentrated on the audio, trying to piece something together. The man had stopped talking, and now they were presumably driving in silence. Rob was still accessing his laptop, entering commands. He swung his laptop into cooperative mode and joined it with Scott's.

"The extra computing power might help." Scott stared at Rob, confused as to what he was doing. He entered a few commands and the sound of the car was suddenly filtered out, exposing some of the background noises they had not heard. Scott rewound the audio back to the point the man was talking. His words were clearer now, and they could almost make them out. Something stood out to Rob. "Doesn't that accent sound familiar?" he pondered out loud. Scott's breath caught in his throat.

"Yes, yes, it does." He could picture the man now, a seedy individual with slicked-back hair and a murderer's smile. This would not be easy if he was involved. Scott ran the voice through a voice-recognition program and compared the recording to the database. Nothing came up, but he was still sure of it. "I know this man, but I can't put my finger on where from." He closed his eyes, recalling memories to sift through to remember the man.

He knew that the man was from the seedy underbelly of town, something he generally avoided, but with a town like theirs it was all too easy to get to. It was the majority of the town. After the local elections had been overturned and the mayor dissolved the town council things started to go wrong. Power had corrupted him, but he had already begun the long spiral down long before.

Nepotism ran rampant in the sections of the local government, promoting his friends and loyal lapdogs over people who really knew what they were doing. As all things do, the jobs didn't get done and the people in power found ways of making it better for themselves. They blamed the collapse of the United States and the dissolution of the UN for most of the problems. Then they began to gather more and more power, trampling the rights of the people in the process. The best part was that the people elected them to do it too. They made no qualms about what they were doing, just like Napoleon was elected emperor of France or Hitler was chancellor of Germany, democracy had reached the generation that was willing to snuff it out in favor of perceived safety.

And like all governments elected to exchange freedom for safety, they exchanged freedom for slavery. Corruption ran rampant in the streets and so did the blood. There was little stability, even now after two years after the coup, and crime still ran rampant. That was why both his apartment complex and hers were gated with electronic security connected to private security firms.

One tended to learn very quickly in the security firms and Scott was no exception. He learned who the people in power were and how to stay away from them—or deal with them when you couldn't. Corporate backing also helped, with the relatively new advanced gear that others couldn't get. And so they found themselves in the mountains, searching for clues with gear that really didn't belong to them.

"Hey, man, we have to figure out what they are saying. I think that's why she turned on her device when she did, or at least got it out to where it could listen." Rob drew him back from his mind, and Scott sighed.

"I know, I was just trying to remember who that was. I definitely know them." Scott frowned, bringing his concentration back to the recording. The voice was definitely clearer but still impossible to make out. Increasing the volume didn't change the ability to hear so Rob pulled up another algorithm to parse the language. The reconstruction began running, attempting to put words together and define the language.

"...she...set back...stall..." The laptop was having problems putting the words together and deciphering them, but it did begin to pull sounds together. Rob and Scott sat back, letting the program run its course. Scott looked up into the sky, staring at the dark canvas of the night scattered with its millions upon millions of stars. Again, wasting time when they needed it the most, but they were stuck at a dead end.

Rob looked at Scott sitting there, staring up at the stars. They had known each other since they were children and he had never seen him like this. He was so much harder than he had been a few short hours ago. Not that he wasn't hard before, it was just different. Someone he loved had been taken from him, and Rob could tell he would do almost anything to get her back, including some very bad things that he never would have done before. Rob hated seeing him like this, he could feel the pain when he talked and could see it when he thought Rob wasn't watching or was so involved he let his guard slip. They had already taken the gear outside of company hours and would likely be reprimanded. He just wished there was someone else they could go to for help. Scott stirred, checked the laptop and went back to looking at the stars.

The stars were one of her favorite things. She was a night owl and loved being up to watch meteor showers and the moon rising. But being able to see the stars made her really happy. She used to say that when she could afford her own place it would be so far out of town she would be able to see the Milky Way strewn across the night sky. Scott himself wasn't too fond of the night, night was filled with darkness and evil hid in the darkness, but he shared her dream of a house far away from civilization. A soft chime alerted them that the program had run its course and they both leaped up, eager to see the results. The transcript floated above the recording's visual readout, and they replayed the audio to compare them.

"...we really don't want to mess this up. If she isn't there in time for tomorrow's ceremony, the entire thing will be set back at least another three days. We might even have to stall for more time, depending on the mood the Duke is in," the voice said. Scott paused the recording.

"The Duke?" Rob wondered, entering the title to search through the known criminal database. "That sounds familiar."

"That's because it is," Scott said. "He operates in the next township over, controlling the slave traffic between the borders." Scott pulled up the files on him, combing through statistics. "That's how I know that voice. The man speaking works as an agent for him in our town. From what anyone has been able to gather he looks clean, but it is more likely that he's a scout who doesn't get involved in the business, merely focusing the muscle on the targets." Rob scanned through the files also, looking for context.

"So he probably lives somewhere relatively close to their hunting grounds, or at least has a base of operations close by," Rob said, sifting through the data.

"Yeah, they have to have something. They were driving an SUV, right?" Scott asked.

"Black, high clearance, rugged. I bet they're way out where no one can get to it," Rob replied, pulling up the satellite maps. Scott nodded, decoupling his laptop from Rob's so they could work independently.

"You work on finding a possible site and I'll keep working on the recording," Scott said. He was fairly certain they had discovered what she had wanted them to find, but kept moving through the recording. He fast-forwarded to the next piece of dialog.

"Where are you taking me?" she asked softly.

"Do not ask questions, do not speak." A different voice answered her, more deep and gruff than the other one.

"I really need to go to the bathroom," she said. There was silence for a while, then she spoke up again. "You don't understand, I need to go really badly, I'm about to—" There was a sharp sound, flesh hitting flesh.

"I told you to shut up," the gruff voice said.

"I'm going to pee my pants," she said. Another slap was heard. Scott felt the heat of anger at the first slap, but now the anger rose through him. He wasn't sure what he was going to do with these people when he found them, but he knew it wasn't going to be good. The audio continued to play, the silence deafening. With the sounds of the car filtered out on the recording only a few sounds remained, the shuffling of clothes as people shifted in their seats, the breathing of everyone in the car. It was surreal. Scott again skipped ahead to the next audio.

"This is an emergency," she said. This time there was no contact, and she stayed silent. Again, the subdued talking from the man they had heard originally. There was another voice responding. Scott didn't need to hear what they were saying to know what they were talking about, it was fairly obvious that they were talking about stopping to let her go to the bathroom. Scott forwarded to the part in the recording with an obvious drop in total noise level. He unfiltered it and replayed it to confirm that it was when the noise of the car dropped off—when they stopped in the valley.

"You have two minutes. Make it quick," the man said gruffly. "Escort the lady to her throne." The second statement must have been directed at his two associates. He heard the sound of the door opening and more cloth movement, sure they were roughly moving her outside, and she protested.

"Remember to keep your hands off her. He wants her intact and pure," the man shouted, presumably from still inside the car. He heard grunts in reply from the muscle. Scott turned off the recording, not really wanting to hear more. The words still rang in his head. Why did he want her intact? Why her and not someone else? The questions rushed through his head, but he really didn't need to know why to stop them and find her. That was what this was about, finding her and saving her. He glanced over at Rob, checking on his progress.

Rob was engulfed in his laptop projection, sifting through maps. The light glow from the laptop bathed his face with a soft light, showing the concentration on his face. He had always been better at electronics than Scott, taking a strong affinity for coding and algorithms at a young age. He had won a middle school coding contest in elementary school, beating out a strong field of competitors all older than he was. And now he was manipulating the map program he had created like a professional violinist plays the violin.

"I have a few sites pre-selected," Rob said, motioning to Scott to come closer. "This is the first one. It's up in the mountains and only accessible by an old logging road. It's a warehouse, probably used to store all the mechanical equipment for the loggers back when they were active. Now it looks like it's abandoned." He flipped the image around and zoomed in on the warehouse.

"When is this image from?" Scott asked. Rob pulled up the details and verified the date.

"Looks like two weeks ago," Rob replied.

"This isn't it, I just listened to the rest of the audio and it looks like whoever took her is also planning on taking her straight to the Duke. This doesn't have nearly enough signs of foot traffic to be the major operating base or headquarters. We have to find something a little more grand." Scott brushed through the image, deleting it off the list.

"Grand, huh," Rob said, pulling up the next location. "How is this for grand?" He flipped it around. It was an impressive building, set high up in the mountains. "It used to be an old ski lodge, a luxury ski lodge. You can see it's seen better times, but it does seem occupied." Scott zoomed into the image. It was three stories tall, a grand entrance overlooking the mountainside below. It did show some signs of wear, crumbling stucco on the sides and loose shingles to name a few. The grandness of it had still stayed though, through the shabbiness, it did look like someone was taking care of it. The grass had not overgrown the main entrance, and the vines looked cut back all along the perimeter. The main courtyard in the back looked like it had been cleaned recently, and it even looked like some of the plants around the area had been tended, albeit poorly.

"How far away is this?" Scott asked. Rob punched in some commands.

"Looks like about an hour and twenty minutes away," Rob replied, reading the output steady on the screen. "But we could make better time cutting through the mountains."

"Wait a second, what is this?" Scott said, pulling the lodge out slightly. He had noticed something when he rotated the lodge around to see the main courtyard in the back.

"That's a wall," Rob said softly. He was right, Scott could see that. It was hidden in the tree line but clearly more recent than the lodge.

"I think we've found our hideout," Scott said softly. He entered a few more commands, bringing up a filtered view of the wall. It stretched around the entire overgrown grounds of the ski lodge, forming an effective compound. He could see watchtowers scattered at strategic locations throughout the wall and the crumbling paved road that led up to the lodge was intersected by a small gate at the foot of the mountain.

"I think you're right," Rob replied. "Here, look at this." Rob rotated the image back up to the lodge. Off to the side was a smaller structure with three garage doors on the side. Rob pointed to the area around both.

"The vegetation is really only cleared out around the main lodge and the driveway, but assuming we know the business of the Duke pretty well, then there isn't really any place for the buyers to go."

"Which means it's only a staging area, or they don't use it for their standard business," Scott replied.

"Sure, but why spend so much money fortifying it, especially as far out as it is? That couldn't have been cheap," Rob said.

Scott didn't reply. Rob was right. There was really no point in spending so much money on a place that was really only a holdover.

"Maybe we don't see the meeting place because it isn't here, or maybe because we just can't see it." Scott knew he had it. "They would know that it would be vulnerable to satellite spying, which is why they built the wall in the trees, and why they made the gate look like it belonged." Scott was right, the gate was built in the same manner as the lodge, grand and a display of money. It was more likely they had built the wall around the old gate than put in a new one.

"They have something underground," Rob said. "This is the perfect place for them. They aren't extremely wealthy from their business but they have money, so they selected something that was out of the way and hidden, both to protect themselves and keep their clientele from being exposed. Of course they would move as much as they could underground, but at the same time they have this lodge as a display of grandness."

"Which tells us something about the Duke we didn't know before," Scott said, contemplating. "He is crafty and intelligent but a fairly newcomer." He looked at Rob. "But I'm sure he feels secure. Why take such a risk to come into our city and compete with all the other drug lords and kingpins?"

"You're right," Rob said, a small grin on his lips. "Secure enough to not expect retaliation, at least not so soon."

"Which means we have the upper hand," Scott said, feeling a small amount of relief.

"Which means we can do it," Rob said.

Chapter Three

They spent the next thirty minutes developing a plan. They pored over the map, noting the weak points and access points.

"Here," Rob said, pointing to the top of the mountain. "This is the last place they expect an attack to take place, and it has the high ground with a clear view of the courtyard. This is where we should attack." Scott shook his head.

"They are almost certainly going to expect something like that and have planned for it. The easiest access point is the road, which means it will be the most fortified. That also works for them because they can then just withdraw to the garage, it completely blocks the sight line of anyone on the ridge." Rob spun the image and noticed what Scott had noticed earlier. The garage was in a straight line up the road to the gate.

"OK, so we hit somewhere else on the wall?" Rob asked, searching for another route to take.

"Yes and no," Scott said. "If we split up, you can take the ridge and draw them out to use the garage for cover. All the muscle will almost certainly fall back to there and anyone inside will prepare for an assault. The most likely places for an assault are the two courtyards." Scott highlighted the two courtyards.

"And they will reinforce the main entrance and probably take some positions in the upper windows for cover," Rob said, adding the schematic overlay of the building they had pulled up from some old files used for permitting that were relatively unsecured. The entrance hall was designed to impress, reaching up to the third floor with sweeping staircases to access each level.

"My money says if an assault is likely they think someone is going to go there," Scott added, "which is why we should choose here." He pointed to the roof on the east wing. "It has access to the third floor from above, which is where I think they would keep her." Rob looked at him with a skeptical look on his face. Scott shook his head. "I just have a feeling about it. If you were an egotistical maniac, wouldn't you keep a prize high up where you were too?" Rob considered it and shrugged.

"Yeah, maybe like a bird in a cage, I get it," Rob said, going back to the image. "But how are you going to get up there?" he asked. Scott pointed to the downspout coming off the gutter.

"They used to make these out of solid metal before everything went to cheap aluminum. Chances are good it still holds up," Scott said.

"Assuming it hasn't rusted out, that's a bit of a stretch," Rob replied. "And then how do you get out once you're in there? That thing won't hold the weight of two, assuming she would go out there with you." Scott went over to their stash of supplies tied to the ATV. He pulled out a rope.

"The old-fashioned way," he said, his face grim. "Using this or wading through blood." Rob could tell how serious he was, and that he would do it if he had to.

"Let's try the rope first," he said wryly. Scott stood there for a moment, then cracked a smile. He realized then how much danger he was putting Rob and himself into, and he knew that Rob had considered it too but never hesitated to help him. Scott put the rope back and looked back up at the stars, longing for his love but knowing that he might lose her and Rob. His heart was torn and Rob must have seen the anguish on his face because he came over and laid a hand on his shoulder.

"You can't do this without me," Rob said quietly. Scott knew, but he almost broke down then.

"Rob, you're my best friend," Scott said to him, suddenly turning toward him. They looked at each other for a second then, really thinking about what this meant.

"And if I wasn't your best friend, I wouldn't be here," Rob replied. "You mean the world to me, and she is important to you so that means she is important to me." Rob came over and held out his hand. Scott clasped his forearm and reached around to bring him into an embrace.

"We'll all get out of this," Scott said. "I promise." He wasn't sure if he could actually make that promise or keep it, but he did anyway. Rob knew that deep in his heart Scott couldn't keep that promise, but he would try as hard as he could to make it true, and he respected and appreciated it from him.

They broke the embrace and got to work. Rob broke down the laptops and checked the weapons and ammunition. New gear was hard to come by after the factory workers rioted and global trade broke down, so they were stuck with 21st-century antiques. Two AR-15s, complemented with a full ammunition loadout, were strapped to the back of the ATV with a broken-down sniper rifle.

A few handguns finished the arsenal, and plenty of magazines to spare. Rob doubted that they wouldn't use the weapons and hoped the reloaded ammunition was still good. Some of it had been done in the warehouse, so he knew that much of it would be reliable, which was something. He picked up the magazine for the sniper rifle and wondered about it. More than a few shots would be bad since it was so much trickier to find good jackets in the same caliber as the larger weapons.

Scott stood with the locket in his hands for a few more moments as Rob went over to check the ammo. He stared at the picture of them in the locket. He didn't want to get it done, a framed portrait, but she had insisted. He was glad she did now, at least for the ability to remind him of who they were. They were a team and had been together for a long time, first as friends. They had grown up together, her, Rob, and Scott. They were always close, being from the same block, and had grown up in a relatively comfortable area. Since they had stuck together, it was natural that something more blossomed between them. Rob had never really been interested in Briana and was supportive when they had told him they were going to start dating in high school. They graduated and he had gone to do his thing while she went to college.

They had been dating for three years when he gave her the locket, and she had pushed him to get a professional portrait. They had had to travel to the next largest city in the region on an armored convoy to even get it done, where they still had photographers. It had been a short weekend getaway, romantic for the time they were together considering how the world had turned out.

He had just started his training but he had already hardened enough to not want to go, but she had pushed him and they got to experience a better time. The thing he had noticed the most was the security. It wasn't that the wall they had built around the city was massive, it was only a six-foot-tall chain-link fence, but the security was everywhere.

It seemed like there was a guard for every five people, and they had passed patrols that were outriders in the surrounding farmland. It was odd seeing old suburbs turned into farmland, they had left some of the better-built houses standing so you could see clusters of them. Others were demolished to the foundation and stacked with containers filled with peas and carrots and squash, with the once grass-covered yards filled with corn and wheat reaching high into the sky. The local market was their destination, bustling with civilians and guarded by many guards.

The stall she had pulled him into was tucked back into the corner and out of the way. Although the technology had advanced at a serious pace, most of it had been wiped out. The man at the small pull-out desk was cheery and plump and had sat them both down in mis-matched stools at the back. He took their photo, all the while talking about his four grandchildren and how fast they were growing and the weather and all the raiders attacking the outbuildings and farms scavenging for food. Scott had been uncomfortable the entire time, especially while they had waited for the photo to be laser transferred onto the locket. The process had made them seem as if they were three-dimensional, which was a little bit disconcerting considering it looked like the upper half of the two of them were floating on air.

The picture was now more comforting to him, allowing him to remember that weekend, how they had picked up market food and had eaten it together sitting on a rock in a small park tucked back from the bustle of the city. The park was no longer tended by anyone but the locals and had taken on a life of its own, mostly overgrowing everything. But you could tell some spots were still being cared for, like the patch around the small stream.

Someone had planted lilies just outside the shade of an old willow tree. He had kissed her there beneath that willow tree, smelling the sweet scents of spring wafting through the park with the stream trickling merrily in the background. It had been like the world was paused as they shared that moment. Scott breathed in, trying to remember the smell of the park, but he smelled only the earthy smell of the trees and stinging of dust. Although he loved being in the mountains, it ripped him from his good memories into the present, leaving the past behind. The emotions didn't leave though, they merely mixed with what was already in his head, sloshing around together into one confusing mess. He pushed the entire thing into the back of his mind, there would be plenty of time to let it all out later, and hopefully later tonight.

"All right, let's get going," Scott said, packing up the last of the ATV. Rob nodded and hopped into the second seat. This particular model had been designed for two riders, plus all the gear associated with them. It had been made for hunting and modified once it was repurposed for the company. Scott started it up, and Rob brought up the map on his laptop display, calculating the optimal route and double-checking using the satellite display.

"We should park the ATV here," Rob said, pointing to a spot just down the mountain on the leeward side. It was surrounded by trees and would be well hidden. "I would have at least two access routes along here and here." He noted a short outcropping that allowed him to scale down to the ATV site and a far easier path through the trees from the peak. "You would also have a far easier time escaping through the gate if you needed to." Scott looked at Rob with a dubious look.

"You want me to go through the most fortified place they have?" he asked. Rob tapped his head.

"No. It will probably be abandoned once they realize the attack is coming from where I'm at. Anyway, it's just a thought. There are plenty of other ways out of there, and hopefully none of them involve a body bag," Rob said, shuffling through the different filters on the map, looking at contours and then shifting to infrared and then back to satellite. The different overlays disconcerted Scott, casting an eerie glow. The dull green of the infrared really set him on edge, somehow making the lodge look haunted.

"Can you put that away?" Scott said. Rob gave him the look.

"No way, I need to know the terrain. Just drive, will you?" Rob said, continuing to go through the different filters and rotating the map. Scott started up the ATV, realizing he was trying to stall unconsciously. He still had his doubts about if they were going to be able to pull this off, but he knew he couldn't fail. Briana was depending on it.

He pushed down on the throttle, starting the ATV with a sharp jolt, not making Rob very happy. Rob made his displeasure known in a few colorful curses combined with a couple of choice gestures and settled back in his seat, researching. The mountainous terrain proved difficult to deal with and took more of Scott's concentration than he was anticipating. The autopilot feature on the ATV was completely useless in the off-road condition they were in so it was fully manual the entire time. He kept it in normal mode, preferring the purr of the engine to keep him company. About halfway through their trip he heard Rob exclaim excitedly.

"Oh yes, this is really good," Rob said.

"What?" Scott replied. A giant grin was on Rob's face, beaming from ear to ear.

"They have a network that's connected to the Internet," Rob said. Scott also began to smile. If there was anything that Rob really liked, it was hacking into places he really didn't need to be.

"Anything else good?" Scott asked. Rob was executing commands at light speed, scrunched down over his laptop. He didn't respond at first, hard at work.

"I'm not sure, I have to get in first. It looks like they have mediocre security, they're running two updates behind," Rob continued to work, executing commands in the dark. Scott let him work in silence, continuing the bumpy drive through the mountains. He could tell they were getting closer to the lodge so he cut the engine to silent mode and the noise virtually ceased. A small whisper was all he could hear due to the noise of them cutting through the air. They were getting closer, and the closer they got, the more nervous Scott became.

"Talk to me, Rob," Scott said. Rob was pulled out of his laptop and finally acknowledged the existence of the real world.

"Well, I have some very good news," Rob said. "They have two automated turrets that I think I will be able to hack. They opted for the latest models on the black market but failed to realize they need enough computing power for targeting that they had to connect it into their net-sphere, which is fairly extensive for what I was expecting." Rob rubbed his hands with glee. "But the best part is that they had to connect their laptops into the net-sphere to avoid self-targeting with the turrets. Which means we know where they all are."

"Which means we know where some of them are," Scott corrected him. "There's no guarantee that all of them keep their laptops on them, or that in the confusion they won't forget to bring them out to a friendly firefight."

"Right, I guess that would make sense. Still, that is quite an advantage. We get to take out their main firepower and know where they are? I'll take that one any day," Rob said. Both of them were elated. They had been going into this blind but now had a good idea of what they were up against, and really had a fighting chance. Even if Rob was unable to hack their turrets and use them against them, he would almost certainly be able to damage them beyond repair, which would demoralize their enemy and make it even easier to get into the lodge, even if they didn't have the advantage of seeing where they all were.

They were about half an hour out when Rob asked him to pull over. Scott looked at the time, it was 3 o'clock in the morning and he could feel himself getting tired as the adrenaline started to wane. He pulled out a pouch from a saddlebag on the ATV filled with coffee and downed it, giving another one to Rob.

"Nothing like freshly bagged coffee to keep you going," Rob said snidely. He ran a hand through his hair, waiting for one of his programs to get through running. He still hadn't gotten far into their system and had to reroute half of his dummy net-sphere back in his apartment to run computing power on the task.

"Does it normally take this long to crack mediocre security?" Scott asked.

"Well, I ran into a few problems," Rob replied sheepishly. "It turns out they probably weren't two updates behind on their security. In fact, they might have had a dummy network set up as a honey trap I might have accidentally spent time hacking into. The good news is that they didn't sever all ties between the two like they should have."

Scott idled the ATV, sitting back in the driver's seat. He knew it was more than likely that Rob would be able to crack their security in less than an hour. In the meantime Scott pulled out his laptop and flipped through the security scans Rob had taken of the net-sphere. It did look pretty impressive, the computing power had to be pretty large to have this big of a net-sphere, so it must not have been cheap and must be running over forty units.

Again, Scott wavered in his resolve. A gang that would have been able to afford that kind of hardware wasn't about to go down easily. Not to mention they were able to make that wall, which probably had a few more surprises in it than they had anticipated.

"Aha," Rob said, leaning back in triumph. "I'm in. I was able to break in at a choke point in the network."

"There has to be more to this wall," Scott said, partly to himself.

"Huh?" Rob said. Scott didn't respond right away, searching through the repository of information Rob had just unlocked. The net-sphere was open to them now, and they were able to pass through it, masked by programs of Rob's making that made them invisible to anyone trying to detect them.

Scott wasn't sure exactly how it worked, but so far nothing was slamming them out of the net-sphere, which was prone to happen if you went snooping around where you weren't supposed to. It looked like they kept some meticulous books on their business as he stumbled across a stash of accounting files. Nothing on the wall from a quick search, but he had no idea if he even had the right search terms.

"I think there is more to that wall, it can't just be a bunch of rocks. That doesn't really make sense to me. Sure, it's pretty well hidden, but if you have automated turrets, then you probably have more than meets the eye somewhere else, especially since we didn't even pick up the turrets from our sat views." Rob scratched his chin with his left hand, looking contemplative.

"Yeah, I guess you're right, there has to be at least some sort of warning system or something, right?" Rob said. "Anyway, you focus on that and I'll try to figure out what to do with the welcoming committee they have set up for us," Rob said, turning back to work. Again, his hands flew as he executed commands.

Scott paused for a moment, thinking about that. The rumor was the newer models could be controlled using your mind, no need for hand gestures at all. He pushed the thought out of the way, no time to be distracted now. He continued searching for the programs associated with the wall. He tried a few more search terms until he got a hit with security.

The program detailed a process used to detect intruders using pressure. Apparently a wire was buried under the wall that sensed weight, and if anything over about fifty pounds hit it, an alarm would go off and alert the security station, buried deep within the lodge, of the location of the intruder.

"It looks like they have some sort of intruder detection device wired into the wall," Scott said to Rob, momentarily pulling him away from his work. "It works on pressure—hang on, I just had an idea," Scott said. He pulled out a grenade from his pack.

"Whoa!" Rob exclaimed. "How the heck did you get that thing?" he asked.

"Standard loadout, for a counter-raid attack," Scott said. "I have eleven more stashed in my pack right here." He patted a saddlebag straddled in between the seats. "And if I've done my math right, it should be able to exert enough pressure to set off that alarm."

Rob stared at him, dumbfounded.

"You want to use grenades to tell them we're here?" Rob asked.

"Actually, I had something a little different in mind. These particular grenades can be remotely detonated on command. If we were to set them up ahead of time and then wait..." Scott trailed off as he could see the gears in Rob's head turning. It clicked, and he could see the realization on his face.

"And we could make them think they're being attacked by more people than we are. Classic diversion tactic," Rob said, grinning once again. Scott nodded.

"Not to mention the confusion it would cause," Scott added. That was more desirable, the more confusion reigned, the better their chances were. If they could send them into such confusion they started attacking each other, that was the best possible outcome they could have.

"Well then, let me do my part. I think I have just a little bit left to go," Rob said. With an overdramatic flourish he gestured one last time. A red icon on the screen turned green, while another stayed red.

"Hmm..." Rob said, returning to his laptop to enter a new set of commands. "It looks like I can access one but not the other, it might be a different model." Scott checked his watch. 3:30 a.m., early in the morning, and they were running out of time. They still had about a twenty-minute drive just to reach the stash point, not to mention getting into position.

"I think you're just going to have to disable it," Scott said. "We're running out of time." Rob nodded and put his laptop to sleep. He pulled out his cell phone, inserting it into his ear and opening a private channel to Scott. Scott did the same, setting his cell phone into position.

"OK, you get up to that ridge while I set up the grenades," Scott said, checking his watch. "Let's synchronize."

Rob held up his watch, and they both did a quick reload, syncing their watches to the prime standard. They compared them and had the same time down to the second.

"It's going to take at least forty minutes to get into position and set up. Once you give me the go-ahead, I'll try to take out the sentries at the gate first to draw their attention. Hopefully that will pull them all out into the open. They'll probably try to activate the turrets too, so I've already programmed the one I couldn't hack to simulate a jam, and the other one I'll direct harmlessly into the forest," Rob said, pointing to the mountain behind the lodge on the map Scott had pulled up.

"Right, I'll strike here," Scott said, motioning to a quadrant of the wall to the southeast of the lodge, away from the gate. "But I'll have most of my grenades set up on the west side and a few on the north. That will give me quick access to the drainpipe and to the roof. From there, I get in, grab the girl, and get out, hopefully causing enough damage to make them rethink their occupation."

He tightened his backpack. Scott had shed the Strength suit while searching for the wall information but still had his backpack to run any auxiliary equipment he might need. He added two pistols to his shoulder holsters and filled his quick reload belt with magazines. A boot knife on each ankle and an AR-45 quick-strapped to his backpack rounded out the complement. Rob kept his Strength suit on, preferring the speed to the silent maneuverability. They shared one last look as they prepared mentally.

"Let's do it," Rob said.

Chapter Four

They reached the stash point in total silence, the ATV motor quiet in silent mode. Scott parked the ATV and turned it off, glancing at his watch. 4:12 in the morning. From the distances they had calculated from the map it would probably take Rob a half hour to get into position and another ten to set up and Scott about forty minutes to plant all the grenades, making his final way to his assault point in about another ten minutes. Scott cinched up his backpack, adjusting all the gear and laying his hands on every weapon to ensure it was secure. They had decided to have Scott loiter for a few minutes to give Rob a head start, just in case he needed any overwatch.

Rob verified the diagnostics were accurate on his Strength suit, slapping his laptop into the interface companion point. After verifying all systems were green, with the exception of a small error readout on his left knee that really wasn't affecting its operation and was just a small warning, he did the same. He strapped the sniper rifle and the remaining ammunition onto his back and slung an AR on his left shoulder, with a few pistols strapped to his belt. Scott had taken the majority of the pistol ammunition while Rob retained most of the automatic rifle ammo. Scott was going to be in closer combat if he did run into any trouble, while Rob needed the firepower to draw them all to his position. While Rob was going over his suit Scott set up a private encrypted channel between them, routing it at minimum power. They were able to converse now, in whispers or shouts, and their cell phones they had put in their ears would detect the sound and automatically adjust it to conversational level.

"Test, 1, 2, 3," Scott said at an extremely low whisper.

"Read you loud and clear," Rob replied, still verifying his readout. Scott leaned back in the driver's seat and kicked his legs up onto the steering handlebars, settling in. It only took Rob a few more minutes to prepare and he flashed Scott a smile and a wave and said quietly, "See you on the other side." And was gone into the night. Scott heard him as he made his way through the woods, even at its quietest a Strength suit wasn't exactly stealth equipment, but Rob was surprisingly quiet other than the snapping of twigs. Scott waited on the ATV, calm on the outside but a raging storm of emotions on the inside.

He was scared, yes, but not really as much as he expected he would be going into so much danger. He was angry, both at himself for letting Briana get taken and at those who had taken her. He was mostly scared of not getting to her in time, that they had done something to her or had hurt or killed her. He wouldn't be able to handle it if she had been hurt. Trepidation for what he was about to do sneaked into his mind. They had no idea how many men the Duke had, but it was more than likely greater than two, which meant odds were not in their favor. Even the acts of divine intervention with the turrets and finding Briana's locket in the middle of the forest barely put them within arm's reach of pulling this off. He had training, true, but they were going up against hardened criminals, likely criminals before the great collapse even happened.

Scott set an alarm for ten minutes from the current time. He stared into the trees trying to keep calm. He used a technique to focus his mind he had learned from Dave. Breathe in for four seconds. Hold for four seconds. Breathe out for four seconds. Hold for four seconds. Repeat. The breathing exercise helped him keep calm, connecting his subconscious to his conscious thought. His heart, on the other hand, beat as fast as it wanted or needed when it was filled with adrenaline. As he gained control of his emotions he became more aware of how tired he was. He had gotten up early at four to prepare for the morning shift, so he had been awake a full 24 hours. He allowed himself to drift off into sleep, a small catnap before the big event. The veterans on the team had told them they all did it if they were preparing for a large confrontation with little sleep. It helped focus the mind to destress.

He was awoken by his alarm softly chiming in his ear a few minutes later. He decided to check in with Rob.

"Rob, how's it going?" he asked softly. They had parked far enough away to not be within earshot of anyone who happened to be close to the lodge but he didn't want to take any chances.

"Doing good, man, I'm scaling the cliffs now. You might want to start moving into position, the terrain north of the lodge is pretty nasty," Rob said at a normal conversational level. Scott had to remind himself that Rob was probably talking very quietly, it had an odd effect on one's brain to talk in a private channel.

"OK, I'm moving out," Scott replied. He checked his gear one last time, a nervous habit, and began to move closer to the lodge. He had an overlay on to augment his vision, added to his vision using an augmentation visor.

Scott had integrated his laptop with his backpack, quadrupling the computing power and adding additional features to the rest of his suit. Even though he had abandoned most of his bulky Strength suit, he kept a few key pieces of hardware to make life easier, the visor being one of them. Well, maybe not that easy. Now the distance to the lodge and direction were highlighted in red on a night-vision overlay in his immediate field of view, giving him a much easier time locating the wall. He started heading east, trying to make his way to the wall.

Staying quiet in the middle of a forest was proving to be difficult. Dead leaves crunched underfoot every time he stepped, and dried twigs cracked every other. Scott almost found himself wishing for rain to cover up the sounds of his movements, then quickly thought better of it. Even so he glanced into the sky, noticing that the stars were now covered with large, ominous clouds that screamed rain at him. That was the last thing he needed right now. He continued through the forest, watching the distance to the lodge count down steadily. He knew that at about 50 yards the wall was set into the slope. At around 75 he noticed it.

It was a wall. Made of interlocking stones, it was clear that no professional had taken part in its construction. The gaps between the rocks were irregular and filled with mortar, some parts even now flaking off and obvious at this distance. Some rocks had even crumbled off the top, although Scott supposed that could have been a ploy to make it seem older. He doubted it though, it was probably shoddily built. Scott moved up into the shadow of the wall and then began heading north, careful not to touch it lest he accidentally set off some alarm he didn't want to.

Along the approach, he had checked carefully for booby traps but had seen none. Apparently they were secure enough in the defensive measures they had put into place to not add more. Granted, that would mean more money and they probably liked to spend their money on something more fulfilling, like booze and drugs. Scott grimaced and continued down the wall. Best not to think of what would happen with a bunch of drugged-up, drunken gang members around Briana.

Something kept nagging in the back of his head though, about the recording. Yes, they had hit her, but it seemed like they were keeping her safe at the same time. She was able to get the locket out of her shirt so that probably meant her hands were free, it took both hands just to activate the thing, and Scott knew it wasn't easy. When she had modified it, she gave it to him to try, and it took him probably twenty tries to start it up.

Granted, he had meaty sausage fingers that were ill-equipped to manipulate small things, which was why she had laughed when she snatched it out of his hands to stop the recording with a small twist of the hinge. Scott shook his head, sending the memory off somewhere else. It was best to concentrate on this, he felt like something big was at the bottom of it. If they had captured her to traffic her as a sex slave, they wouldn't have treated her nearly as nicely. In all likelihood they would have stuffed her in the trunk, maybe having their way with her beforehand. It was part of the job. But she had been deliberately set inside the car where the others were, and it sounded like the leader was...

That had to be significant. And then they had stopped for her to go to the bathroom. That was very surprising. Why would they stop to let her go to the bathroom when it was more likely she could get away? The risk just wasn't worth the reward. She had to be special somehow, probably special to the Duke in some way.

Scott stumbled in a drop he hadn't seen since he was thinking and not paying attention to his surroundings. He caught himself before he fell down the embankment he was descending, cursing himself in the process. This was no time to get careless, he wasn't sure what he was thinking. So what if she was special to the Duke, she still was taken by these creeps and he was about to save her from them, no matter how special she was to them. He focused now, making his way quickly and quietly along the wall, which was free of noisy leaves and twigs. He made it to his first implantation point. He pulled out a grenade from his backpack and twisted it, setting it to remote detonation and buried it carefully into a crevice between two rocks. He began to make his way to the next point, fully focused on the task at hand when he heard Rob's voice speak in his ear.

"All right, Scott, I'm set up and ready to go here. I've got a good vantage point on the lodge." Rob was measured and calm. "It looks like I have about three bozos out now, two at the front gate and one patrolling the area around the lodge, although the more I look at him the less patrolling he seems to be doing and the more smoking he does. The two by the gate are definitely relaxed and having a good time."

"Roger that," Scott said quietly, planting another grenade softly into the wall about five yards from the last one. The rocks were covered with moss and slippery in the morning dew and Scott had to carefully place them to keep them from falling down into the ground beneath the wall. He wasn't sure if that would affect the pressure wave from their blast setting off the alarm but he would rather not take his chances. "I have about eight more grenades to plant and then I'll be ready to go after I make my way to the other side."

"Got it, I'll sight in and make sure these bozos don't get out of my sight. It is pretty early," Rob said. Scott glanced down at his clock. 5:02. Early enough to keep out most of humanity but not the early risers.

He just wished that they had had a pretty rough night last night and were all trying to sleep off the booze. It was the only thing that was plentiful anymore. He made his way another five yards and got another grenade out to plant it. He glanced up into the sky again, night was still deep over the world but those clouds looked ominous still. Another wave of fear and doubt came over him, washing him into a dark place, as dark as the clouds above him.

"Rob," he whispered softly.

"Right here, man," Rob said. Just hearing his voice made him feel better. Scott pulled himself together and continued forward another eight yards, planting another grenade into the wall. Another few yards, another grenade. He forced himself to keep going, picturing Briana's face in his mind. He had to do it for her, he knew he was her only hope left in the world.

Suddenly, Scott heard and felt the crunch of footsteps. Someone was coming his way. Scott pressed himself up against the wall, trying to shrink into the darkness. He could feel the cold stones of the wall on his hands digging into his flesh at the points, as if they were trying to eat the warmth in his body. The footsteps continued to get closer to him, crushing the fragile leaves underneath large feet. Scott slowed his breathing, trying to become as silent as possible and as dark as the night. He had no idea if the person coming was coming for him or coming for some other reason, but he really did not want to find out.

The crunch of leaves under the feet turned into soft claps as they got closer, as if the feet were climbing the wall somehow. Scott realized they were probably going up steps and began looking around to see if there were any handy hiding spots other than right next to the wall they were trying to penetrate. Other than the trees, there really wasn't much. Maybe an old downed tree every once in a while, probably from the construction of the wall, but nothing large and old enough to give much cover.

The footsteps continued to get closer.

Scott continued to look for a way out as panic began to set in. He tried to calm himself again with his breathing exercise, moving his hand to a pistol and wishing he had a silencer. In for four, hold for four, out for four, hold for four. Repeat. He ran over them as he continued to hear the footsteps get closer, and then they stopped. Scott wasn't sure where the person had stopped, so he looked up.

He was staring at a man perched precariously above him, his toes overhanging the edge. Scott watched in horror as the man slung the rifle he was carrying onto his shoulder and reached down toward his crotch.

The man was looking out into the forest, unaware of his presence. Scott heard the zip of a zipper and waited, transfixed, as the man set about to do his business. The man looked down. Something caught his eyes, and Scott found himself looking straight into the man's dark eyes.

He saw them widen in surprise, and the man grunted as the realization dawned on him that he was staring at someone out in the middle of nowhere.

"Change of plans," Scott whispered to Rob as he drew his pistol. The look of surprise turned to panic in the man's eyes and he fumbled, awkwardly trying to zip himself up instead of reaching for his weapon. Scott capitalized on his moment of hesitation.

"What do—" A gunshot interrupted Rob's query as Scott pulled the trigger, aiming for the man's head. The report ripped through the still silence of the night and bounced around the valley and inside Scott's mind. The man stopped moving and fell forward, crashing down onto Scott with the obvious weight of death.

Scott pushed hard on the man, his mind panicking as he tried to get the weight off him. A buzzing sound in his left ear from the gunshot washed over him, and he could feel the bile rising in his throat as the picture of the surprise in the man's face came unbidden to his mind. Scott had never killed a man, and seeing his eyes made it worse. He pushed the man free and quickly turned to the side to throw up as the body tumbled down the small embankment he was standing on.

"Scott, what the hell is going on down there?" He heard Rob's voice come into his mind slowly, like the volume was being turned up from mute as he spoke.

He found it odd as he was bent over, hands on his knees.

"I think I killed him," Scott said, no emotion in his voice.

"Killed who? What do you mean?" Scott could hear the emotion in Rob's voice, somewhat strained. Scott slumped into a sitting position, leaning his back against the wall.

"I killed him," Scott repeated, as much to himself as to Rob.

"Scott, you have to snap out of it. I see two guards headed to the east, you need to get out of there," Rob said. "Get to Briana!" Scott felt a jolt as her name went into his ear. He shook his head, freeing it from the grip of death and got back onto his feet. There was no time to plant more grenades now. Scott pulled up the map in his visor and enabled the entry point display, telling him he was still over 150 meters from his planned entry point.

He started sprinting south, jumping over downed trees and making his way along the wall. He didn't know if they had abandoned the gate, but he was about to find out as he quickly made his way to it. It came up into view and he quickly flashed to an infrared filter. It lit up the two guards like a Christmas tree in his vision.

"Rob, I need you to draw their fire, right about now," Scott said in a whisper between his labored breaths. "I need a little overwatch."

"I got you," Rob said. A gunshot rang out and one of the bodies crumpled in his view. The other started and jumped behind cover, concealing himself from Rob's line of fire in a makeshift shack cobbled together out of stone by the gate. The tree line broke as he neared the gate, a meadow with a rocky outcrop in the middle cut in half by an old crumbling road. Unfortunately he still had a good view of Scott's line of where he was going to run. Scott cursed and continued running, attempting to get by him before he had a chance to shoot. Unfortunately the man saw him and swung his weapon around, sending off three shots in quick succession. Scott dropped down low and slid behind a large rock outcropping, hearing the bullets whiz by his head.

"Uh oh," he heard Rob say in his ear.

"That doesn't sound good, Rob," Scott said, putting his pistol back into the holster and unstrapping the AR from his backpack. He peeked around the side of the rock and pulled back quickly as the man in the guard shack shot at him.

"Not good at all. It looks like we have company. I see four...no, six men coming your way in a hurry. And I've got about five shooting at me. I don't understand—why don't they all go to you so you can have the fun." Scott heard the sound of gunfire to the north, and then a rapid spin-up of a turret with quick shots ringing out from it. The scattering of shots sounded like a conglomeration of weapons, likely personal guns paid for by the Duke's pockets.

"Tell me you have control of that turret," Scott said, glancing around at the terrain. The foundation of an old building lay a few yards away from him and he was glad he hadn't fallen in the hole it made. Other than that he was on open ground, no trees for quite a few yards. He wasn't sure what he could use to his advantage but he did know one thing, he was trapped right here for the time being. He checked his grenades as Rob said to him.

"I have control, don't worry." A louder shot from the sniper rifle rang out over the sound of gunfire and Scott heard a man scream in pain. More cursing followed from the other members of the ragtag gang army, none of it pretty. Scott set his four grenades back in his pack and attempted another look around the rock. Again, bullets met him so he pulled back, but not before getting a camera shot off of his own.

He pulled up the photo, wiping away a small amount of blood from a small cut on his cheek, probably from rock shrapnel of a bullet ricochet. He could tell that some of the men had made it to the guardhouse, at least three of them, maybe all six even. They had taken up defensive positions and there was no way Scott was going to be able to get a shot off without taking a few bullets back, and the more chances he took the more likely those bullets were going to connect. He was only a few yards away from the gatehouse, close enough to be within throwing distance but he didn't want to use his grenades since they weren't going to be able to take out all of them at once.

"Do you think a distraction might help?" Scott asked Rob, racking his brain on what to do to get out of his pinned-down position.

"I think it might be a little bit late, or maybe it's too early," Rob replied, another sniper shot ringing out above the noise. "I've got them pretty well distracted as is right now, but the more shots I take the more likely they are to find me." Rob had fallback positions set up already but it was too early to use them, they were hoping for more time for Scott to search the lodge instead of Rob continually falling back. Eventually he would be overwhelmed, if they chose to send men up the embankment. I'm going to need a bomb to distract these guys, Scott thought to himself. A light bulb went off in his mind.

"Hey Rob, how many got to my position?" Scott asked, not daring to go in for another look. He could hear them yelling at him to surrender now.

"Probably eight. It looks like they've fully mobilized now, the first couple came out in their underwear. It would have been comical had they not been sending hot lead my direction." For a moment Scott had the picture of men in underwear carrying weapons over their heads rushing out into the night and couldn't help himself but chuckle.

"All right, well, I'm going to draw as many of them to my position as I can. I have an idea," Scott said, pulling off his backpack and grabbing the AR. He grabbed a grenade and lobbed it over the outcrop in the general direction of the gate, and felt very satisfied as he heard multiple people yelling grenade.

He waited the five seconds for it to activate, and then as soon as it went off with a satisfying bang, he popped his head out from behind the rock and began shooting in the general direction of the gate. He wasn't really planning on hitting anyone, but he heard a few cries of anguish and then pulled himself behind the rock as they returned fire.

"Yep, I think that's going to help with your plan," Rob said dryly. "You have another four boogies headed your way from the lodge. These look pretty well equipped, let's even the odds a little." Another sniper rifle shot rang out and another cry of anguish mixed in with the random scattering of gunshots and yelling. "Make that three—where do they get these guys?"

"Nice job," Scott said.

"I'm shifting positions. I think they're going to find out pretty soon that their turrets have been compromised. I'll see if I can employ it now," Rob said.

"Hold off on that until my signal," Scott said.

"Signal?" Rob asked.

"You'll know."

"...OK, moving," Rob said.

Inside was a mini power supply with a large concentration of power. Scott used to have to do calculations of how much energy was stored in it in his high school science class, which he did not appreciate until now. He knew that there was enough energy in one of the Strength suit backpacks to send its wearer a half a mile into the air if fully discharged at once, which would make a tidy bomb.

Why anyone would willingly strap a bomb to their back he had never known until he tried one on and put it through the paces. He had gotten used to that bomb and eventually learned how to short it out during his maintenance training sessions purely by accident. The instructor had been livid, after quickly reversing what he had done, and gave him an ass chewing he still felt to this very day. Maybe that was what had seared the memory into his brain, but he took off the access cover and began to go through the process.

He slid himself into a sitting position and pulled out a small flashlight off of his belt. This was not something you did in the dark. Scott wasn't sure if they would be able to see the light from where they were at, but he didn't want to risk it so he turned it on in medium-level red. It gave him enough illumination to make out the circuitry clearly enough for what he was about to do. The familiar mass of wires and circuit boards met him, after spending hours in the machine shop he finally learned how to do his own maintenance. As he concentrated, thoughts of that time came unbidden to his head.

At first he had no desire or interest to maintain his own equipment. He thought it was a waste of time to have to clean and service his gear, especially his Strength suit, when there was a contractor much better and faster at it than he was, but Dave made him go through the course anyway.

"Go through the course," he had said, as if Scott was a child. "And we'll see how you feel after you complete it." That experience had altered his perception of the job. At first it was tedious, and his large fingers made him feel clumsy and unsuited for the job. He wasn't able to get into some of the small spaces as easily as some of the other students had, but he had told Dave he would at least finish the course, so he pressed on. Every morning they learned about the circuitry and mechanics of the suit, and some technical knowledge he really didn't understand very well, and then they set about overhauling their suits in the afternoon and evenings.

He learned about the linear actuators and piezoelectrics that helped harvest the energy from his movements to convert them to electrical signals to then maneuver the suit. He learned about the web of sensors that gave the suit almost as much sensitivity as his own skin to be able to react to impact appropriately. And he learned about the neural web that was connected to the backpack to draw its power from.

As far as he knew, the backpack wasn't exactly cold fusion, the radiation emitted from something like that would have killed anyone who was close enough to be wearing it on their back. But it was a form of nuclear reaction that was able to almost completely harvest the energy from the bonds and convert it directly to electricity.

The reactions were only initiated as the suit demanded the electricity, and could respond quickly to ramp up to full power if needed. The physics of it was a little beyond him, but if you short-circuited the demand relay, the reactions proceeded to full power in about 30 seconds and if you let it go any farther than that you had a small bomb on your hands. When he completed the course he was able to break down the suit and replace anything in less than a day. He could also trust his suit more and was able to push it to limits he had never even known existed. After that Dave began to show him some pretty incredible things he could do with it and he had never doubted him again, and had to eat his own words.

Scott pulled out the power regulation circuit card from its chassis and carefully pried open the demand relay. He tuned out the sounds of the battle behind him, focusing solely on what he was about to do next. He very carefully pulled out the regulation chip, being extremely careful not to bend any contacts. He reversed it 180 degrees and put it back onto the board, clicking it back in place with a satisfying snap. He then pulled a diode from the board and reversed it as well, being extremely careful not to break it. A few bullets whizzed overhead, momentarily breaking his concentration. Apparently his new friends didn't like him ignoring them.

"Hey Rob, can you pin down the group at the gate for a few seconds, or at least force them back into cover?" Scott said quietly.

"Roger that, buddy," Rob said. "I'm running low on ammo, but I can make it happen." Sniper rifle shots rang out, and Scott heard at least one scream—the man screaming about his leg being hit. The commotion allowed Scott to concentrate again, and he slid the circuit board back into place. He glanced at his watch, timing down the seconds until he was ready to go, and eyed the small foundation. He hoped that the combination of the rocky outcrop and depression in the ground would keep him safe from a majority of the concussion wave that he was about to throw into the world. He hoped it would. Scott watched ten seconds count down and he said a quick prayer.

The next few moments were the longest in his life. Scott sprang up and tossed the backpack over the outcrop, aiming to land in front of the gate, knowing he had about ten seconds until it detonated. In his mind he began a countdown.

9. He turned and sprinted toward the foundation, briefly coming out from behind cover.

8. He was in full view of the guards at the gate.

7. He heard one shout as he was halfway to cover.

6. He continued to sprint, speeding up as fast as he could run.

5. He could almost see them all turn their weapons toward him in his mind's eye and level them at him.

4.

The bullets began to fly, buzzing dangerously close past him.

3.

He ducked into a slide, feeling the dry ground begin to burn away the flesh on his now exposed flesh, glancing back to see his backpack had landed squarely in the middle of the group of guards.

2.

He dropped into the hole of the foundation, a hollow thump running through him as his chest hit the dirt.

1.

He plugged his ears and opened his mouth.

0.

For a second, the world stopped.

Nothing.

"Huh," Scott thought, "I guess I miscalc—"

An explosion triggered.

If you were staring down at the lodge from the air, as if you were a bird or in an airplane, and the world was operating in slow motion, you would have first noticed a blinding flash from the backpack that had landed squarely in the midst of about ten gang members, being picked up by one that not-so-lucky bastard. The shock wave followed the flash, instantly killing the majority of the guards in the blast radius and knocking the ones that survived back a few feet to slam into whatever hard item they happened to connect with.

From there the shock wave spread out in a neat little dome, striking the group of guards taking cover behind the garage and knocking them forward into the wall. It hit the remaining windows in the lodge and garage and bowed them inward until the stress was too much and the glass cracked and then shattered, caught up on the wave and blowing inward. The shock wave passed over Scott as he lay in the hole, for the most part, but it did let him know it was there with a little pat on the back. It continued into the trees, ripping into the closest ones and shaking the ones farther out. The sonic boom followed the wave, bursting the eardrums of anyone still alive.

"Holy crap," Scott heard Rob say through the ringing in his ears. "That is one hell of a grenade." Shaken from the remnants of the explosion, Scott knew he had to act fast or he would lose his one chance at capitalizing on the chaos that would ensue.

He unsteadily rose to his feet, seeing the destruction his bomb had created. There was now a crater where there once had been an impressively decaying gate. Bodies were strewn haphazardly around it, some still moving but most still. He was glad it was still night, which covered up the details that weren't illuminated by the moon. Scott turned and ran west, heading to the other side of the compound.

"Well, I'm moving," Rob said. "That gives me a break."

"I think now might be a good time to activate that turret," Scott said to Rob, still struggling to recover. His legs felt like jelly and his head was pounding. Still, he knew that chaos was going to be their friend.

"Yeah, I'm on it," Rob said. A few moments later Scott heard the turret chatter back into life and then heard cries of anguish as he assumed it turned on its former master. As he ran he rationalized with himself. These were bad people who stole women from their homes, and probably young girls too.

They don't deserve to live.

But something inside him fought that, they were still people, and he really didn't have the right to take them out of this world. Briana came to his mind once more, her face plastered in his mind's eye. She was what he was doing this for. His legs steadied up as he ran, quickly approaching his destination. There was a low spot in the wall over here, and he quickly climbed into the tree that had a branch overhanging the wall. While still in the tree he pulled up his laptop.

"Are you in position?" Scott said to Rob.

"Yeah, setting up now," Rob replied.

"OK, I've got one more distraction for us," Scott said. He accessed the remote detonation feature of the grenades and set them to detonate in 15 seconds. Putting his laptop away he jumped from the branch over the wall and broke his fall into a roll on the other side. Scott saw the old gutter on the side of the lodge, and it looked, thankfully, intact.

His legs still radiated pain from the burns he had collected on his little stunt to blow up everything to kingdom come, but he ignored it as he continued up to the lodge, moving more slowly this time. He heard the distant explosions as the grenades detonated and hoped that that would confuse them even more. Chaos, again, was their friend, and he hoped they had heaped it on them. "How are we looking?" he asked Rob.

"Well, I have more bad guys exiting the lodge from the front and back doors, but I'm still not sure how many are inside. That bomb you made was pretty effective, it looks like they only had two survivors at the gate, and I let them drag them to cover. The five behind the garage don't seem to want to fight as much either since I turned the turret on them," Rob replied. "I think you're going to have a clear path; the reinforcements seem to be heading to the east toward your distraction."

Another sniper shot rang out and a clatter of automatic fire followed. "I think the rest are going to bottle up and hold out, assuming they have more people."

"They will," Scott said, stealthily making his way up the slope. There was little here for cover for him to hide behind, the overgrowth ran thick but not high enough to hide him. He only had about ten yards to go, and he was keeping a close eye on the windows to make sure no one was watching. He was fairly sure that they were distracted enough to be focused on the other side of the lodge, but if they were professionals, which they seemed to be, they would have lookouts checking all around them.

Scott made it to the wall of the lodge and carefully checked for any traps before placing his hands on the cold metal of the downspout. He was relieved to have it feel solid in his grasp. He reached higher and put one foot and then the other so that he was hanging in midair off the downspout. Scott felt it give a little, but it held and he steadily made his way up the downspout.

He felt like the spider in the nursery rhyme, just waiting for the metal to give a little bit too much and wash him back out. Scott didn't know if he would be able to try to climb back up, though. He passed by the second floor. His hands began to ache, trying to hold on to a thick metal pipe was not easy so he had to dig his hands into the brick wall behind it to find a perch.

He gave up trying to put his feet on the pipe, they kept slipping off, so he just used the brick to push himself up. Luckily his shoes were relatively new and had a good grip. He passed the third floor. He kept looking up as his arms began protesting, not used to supporting his weight on just his arms.

Only a few more feet and he could grab the roof to pull himself up.

He continued, one leg over the other, one hand releasing and then reaching. Finally, he found himself within reach of the roof. He pushed himself up on his right foot and grabbed the roof, and then felt his right hand slip as the roof tile came off in his hand. His foot slipped and he desperately clutched tightly with his left hand as his foot and arm careened into the void.

He managed to ~~hold~~ on, but he saw the loose roof tile fall in slow motion to the ground, shattering into pieces. The sound was distinct, but he hoped it would be lost in the continuing chorus of the firefight. He pulled his right hand back to the roof and grabbed it again, this time finding solid purchase.

His right foot sought its way back from oblivion and connected with the side of the wall, and he pushed with his foot far enough to reach his elbow over the roof. He pulled himself up as he quickly surveyed the roof and found it empty. He strained, pushing his heavy body up on weak arms, and collapsed onto the roof.

He lay there for a few moments on his back, looking up at the sky filled with clouds. Occasional flashes of light from the gunfire flashed to his right, hidden by the lodge but still straining to be seen. As his breathing began to slow and the adrenaline died down, Scott could feel the pain returning to his legs and the protesting of his muscles became evident.

His arms screamed at him, not happy for putting him through that. He was still carrying his belt with two pistols and the rope and automatic rifle slung on his back, and it had not been easy to haul them up with him. He recovered a little from it and then forced himself to sit up.

"I'm on the roof," Scott said softly.

"I don't mean to kill the mood, but you may want to hurry up a little," Rob replied. Another sniper rifle shot rang out. "I'm out of bullets for this thing. How important is it to bring it back?" he asked.

Scott snorted. He could see Dave having a bit of a meltdown but knew that he would rather see him alive without it than dead.

"If you can bring it, I would. That thing is worth a lot," Scott replied. Standing, he knew that he would have to travel to the other side of the roof and drop down to a balcony conveniently located on the third floor. He carefully made his way across the tile roof, stepping gently so that his feet did not make a sound on it.

It was excruciatingly slow going, but he resisted the urge to speed himself up. He had learned long ago that the more rushed you were the more likely it was you were going to screw it up. As he padded across the roof the gunfire grew more and more infrequent. Scott could hear the occasional chatter of the weapons and a returning burst of the automatic rifle Rob had no doubt switched to following the exhaustion of the sniper rifle rounds.

He reached the edge of the roof and laid down. Slowly, after drawing a pistol, he edged himself over the gutter, peering down onto the balcony.

It was empty, save for a few old and broken pots. No one was in sight. He could see some of the other balconies on lower floors, probably old suites for the richest visitors, and they too were empty. No light spilled onto the balcony he had chosen, unlike some of the other ones that were flooded with a soft glow. The lodge had lit up like a Christmas tree as soon as the assault started, lights bursting forth in quick succession, and they remained on even now.

Gingerly, he swung himself around and slowly lowered himself to the balcony railing, which appeared to be made of stone. He tested the railing, slowly adding more of his weight, and was satisfied as it held. He lowered himself onto the balcony railing. When it supported all of his weight, he jumped off and softly landed on the balcony itself, freezing in place. He looked around, making sure he had not disturbed anything, the broken pottery safely behind him.

Scott turned his attention to the door, the glass broken from the shock wave of the bomb, mostly on the floor of the balcony. He could now tell he landed right in it, but it had barely crunched at all when his feet hit the floor. From what he could tell there was no one in the room, but he carefully crouched down and tried the doorknob.

It was locked.

Not to be dissuaded, he reached a hand through the now-empty space where the glass had resided and unlocked it from the inside. "Well, that turned out better than I expected," he thought. He stopped for a moment, his hand on the knob, considering what was ahead. Nothing easy, of that he was sure. Fear again coursed through his body, and he brought Briana in front of it. There was no way they had come this far and done this much just to give up. He took a breath, his resolve returned.

"Rob, I'm going inside."

Chapter Five

Slowly, he crept into the room.

The sounds of the battle raged outside, a pitiful firefight being traded back and forth. He closed the door behind him and winced as the door clicked back into place, the sound reverberating around the room like a gunshot in his mind.

He knew that wasn't the case, but the adrenaline and fear mixed with resolve amplified his thoughts and sent them careening around his mind, striking out at whatever came first. He let his eyes adjust, the room darker than outside.

A new sound joined the fray, thunder rolling off in the distance. The clouds outside still loomed, frothing around in the high winds in the sky, the moon behind still casting a warm reflecting glow from the sun.

As his eyes adjusted to the darkness, he began to make out the contents of the room. To his left was a large bed, its legs crumpled from years of un-use, and to his right was a sturdy dresser with a very old TV on top, something he had not heard of in years. Apparently they were in vogue before three-dimensional projection technology became mass marketed. A chair was overturned in the corner, and two doors led out of the room, one on the wall opposite the balcony door he entered from and one just behind the dresser and TV. Feeling the rush of blood in his ears and the pounding of his heart in his head, Scott tried to calm himself enough to listen to the environment around him.

Apart from the random, sporadic gunfire outside, the room was relatively quiet. He could hear the cursing and conversation of some of the injured and alive, presumably hiding behind the garage, but it was muted. He began to stalk his way across the room, gently placing one foot in front of the other. He froze as his foot descended onto the old floor, a loud creaking breaking forth from the joist beneath. He cursed beneath his breath and listened closely for any noises below or just outside the room. Hearing nothing, he began to move again, attempting to not make the old place give him away.

He made it across the room with just a few more creaks and groans from the old building, heading for the door he assumed did not lead to the bathroom. He realized he did not have his pistol out and drew one from its holster, ejecting the magazine and checking the contents of it. Fourteen bullets left. This was the pistol he used earlier against the guard. The memory made him pause, remembering the face of the man he had killed, and in quick succession the sound and pressure of the explosion that took out so many. He quickly pushed them aside and out of his mind and focused on the task at hand. Grabbing the handle, he turned it and quietly opened it, peering outside into the hallway.

At first glance the hallway seemed filled with people, but Scott quickly realized, after a start that sent his heart pumping through the roof, that it was just filled with old, decrepit furniture. He eased his finger off the trigger, the pistol quickly brought up into a shooting position. He relaxed a little bit, bringing the barrel of the pistol down into a carry position. He stood up and made his way out into the hallway, closing the door softly behind him.

Scott realized he had no idea what to do next. They had really only planned getting into the lodge and nothing else above and beyond that. Looking down the hallway, Scott realized there were a lot of doors to check behind.

"Rob, do you have sight on any windows that are lit up?" Scott asked, crouching behind a piece of furniture with a vase on it. At best it was a long shot, since he would only be able to see half the lodge. Based on what they had learned, Briana was important to the Duke, which meant he was going to keep her like a prized possession.

Scott had guessed that either meant the top floor of the lodge, which would be most isolated and able to be protected, or somewhere deeper within the compound underground, which would be harder to search out.

Both Rob and Scott put their money on the third floor, underground would be more complicated to try for and they hoped that wasn't the case. But where exactly on the third floor?

"So, I have a few lights on the first floor and none on the second or third. I can't tell you about the other side," Rob said. "I'm still giving them hell out here, but things are harder. That sniper rifle really kept them pinned down, but my rifle just doesn't have the accuracy at this range, and I'm up against the odds here." Scott could tell there was a note of desperation in his voice, which worried Scott a little, but he knew that rushing into things would make both their lives more difficult—or a lot shorter.

"OK, I'll try the other side." Scott tried to remember if he had seen any lights on his approach, since he had approached from the opposite side Rob had. "Hang in there, Rob, I know you can keep them busy." Scott also knew that the confusion they had probably thrown them into was likely dying out and they were starting to realize things that Rob and Scott did not want them to figure out—like that there was no one assaulting from the east where he had planted the grenades, or that there weren't as many of them as it first appeared.

They were fighting a war of attrition that they could not afford. If either of them were hit, then half their force was gone just like that. Scott had to put himself into the Duke's shoes.

Scott retreated into his mind, only slightly conscious of the real world. If he were the Duke, he would have power—probably a good deal of power based on the amount of men they had seen outside and what he was able to do to kidnap Briana without many clues left behind. So he had power over professional criminals, was in all likelihood in the business of kidnapping and selling women and girls as slaves already, but had treated Briana differently.

Just letting her out of the car to stop would have been out of the question if she wasn't special. So she was special to him, but how? It wasn't because he was a relative, Scott knew all of Briana's male relatives and what they did in general. It was more likely he still wanted her to be a slave—but his slave. That made the most sense to him. So if he wanted her to himself, he was most likely to keep her in the nicest place he had available to him, maybe the biggest room on the floor. They weren't able to get a perfect layout of the lodge, but Scott pulled out his laptop and brought it up, scanning up to the third floor.

There were two larger rooms on the third floor at either end of the hallway. Scott was close to one, and they both were on the side farthest away from Rob's vantage point. Scott turned, looking at what he thought was the closest suite. He tamped out the soft glow of his laptop projection and put it back into the pack on his belt.

The door was plain, but it wasn't ordered in the same manner as the other ones, it looked like it would go to a larger room. He started for the door, rising to his feet and slowly approaching it. The door was large enough that there was no space under it. Scott would have liked to at least have been able to tell if there was a light on in the room or not, but he was going in blind.

"Rob, I think she's in a suite, and I'm approaching one of two on this floor," Scott said, partially trying to convince himself that he was doing the right thing.

"Makes sense to me," Rob replied, the muted sound of gunfire still chattering after a few moments. "Good luck." Scott breathed in and out, calming himself as he approached the door, reaching one hand out with the other hand holding the pistol at chest level, ready to go if needed.

He paused, his hand hovering just above the doorknob, listening closely with one ear nearly pressed up against the door. He did not hear anything and proceeded to grab the handle and twist in one fluid motion, swinging the door open as quietly as the old hinges would allow. He immediately dropped down to one knee, scanning the room from left to right as quickly as he could and assessing the situation.

This room was different from the one he had entered from. This was smaller but had a larger door leading to a different room. Two sofas occupied most of the room, sagging and old, and they were devoid of anyone sitting on them. He quickly made his way behind the door, discovering nothing hiding behind it.

He shuffled right to the door, discovering a very large bed decaying in the second room attached to the first. Again, not one person was in the room. Scott turned around, feeling his heart sink and then hope again. There was still one more room to go. He made his way out of the room slowly after checking all the doors—one to the closet, which was empty, and one to a large bathroom, which also had no one in it.

Once again he turned the handle on the door he had shut on the way in and opened it, making his way out of the room and into the hall.

"I'm hurting here on ammo," Rob said softly in his ear. Scott started at the interruption.

"It might be better to stop shooting and provide some inside information on their net sphere then," Scott replied.

"If I stop shooting they might be suspicious," Rob said. Scott was making his way down the hallway now, carefully approaching the main staircase. If he was going to leave someone to guard the third floor, then that would be his best place to put them. He stuck to the shadows on the edges of the hallway.

"I think it's time to take that chance," Scott said. "I'm going silent for the time being. I'll check in when I think it's clear."

"Roger," Rob replied. "I'll get into that net sphere and feed you some information if I can get it." Scott peered around the corner of the wall and found his suspicions confirmed. A man stood at the top of the landing, crouched behind the banisters. He did not see Scott, as he was currently preoccupied with the sounds of gunfire coming from outside, nervously switching between peering outside and down the stairs.

Scott's guess was that this was one of the newer gang members and was untested in combat. He gauged the distance between the wall he was behind and the wall to the hall where he wanted to go. He knew he either needed to go silently without him noticing or take him out. He prepared himself for the silent trek.

He crept forward, eyes locked on the man. The man was extremely nervous, nearly jumping out of his skin every time a distant burst of gunfire rang out. His attention was still focused outside as Scott made it halfway across the opening. He was nearly three-quarters of the way across when the man's cell phone chirped, a voice drifting out from it.

"All right, kid, we're going to send you out. We have some wounded out here so come down," he said. The man, who had jumped when it rang and dropped his cell phone picked it back up and with shaky hands keyed it.

"I thought I was supposed to stay up here?" he said nervously. Scott held his breath and continued, making his way across the opening, briefly glancing away from the man to see how much distance he had left. Only about two more feet.

"Get your ass down here," the voice said. Scott had his hand outstretched, reaching for the wall of safety. He felt it brush up against it.

"O-okay," the man said, clearly defeated. Scott quietly slipped behind the wall as the man turned back to look behind him, right where Scott was seconds ago. Back pressed up against the wall, Scott stood completely still, pistol in hand and ready for the man to come around the corner.

Scott heard the man move, his clothing brushing by itself, and he heard the footsteps on the floor. He was mumbling to himself, nothing Scott could make out.

Scott held his breath, feeling the adrenaline shoot through him.

He tightened his grip on his pistol, placing his finger on the trigger in preparation.

At first he could not tell if the man was coming his way or down the stairs. The footsteps paused, and Scott heard the man ruffling around, clothing scratching on clothing.

Something shook around, clattering around, and Scott heard the scratch and flare of a match lighting. The man sighed suddenly, and Scott heard him breathe in slowly, probably lighting a cigarette. The man took a long drag and exhaled slowly, then continued walking. Scott forced himself to breathe slowly and quietly.

The sound of footsteps descending down the stairs brought instant relief to Scott. He slowly eased his finger off the trigger, realizing how close he was to squeezing it. One step at a time the man at the top of the stairs got farther away from him, and he could feel the danger descend slowly as well. Scott began to breathe easier, breathing quickly from holding his breath.

"Slowly." His breathing slowed down as he began to recover both his senses and his fear, binding it tightly behind his resolve. He still had his mission, and he would see it through.

The door at the end of the hall began to beckon to him, calling him from the darkness down the corridor. It was more ornate than all the others, he could tell that in the dim light from the window, carvings adorning its wooden frame. Scott crept closer to the door and its alluring quality. He paused, standing at the entrance to it.

Overhead, the clouds roiled and rollicked. They flicked their tongues of lightning at each other, striking the trees in the forest and cracking them in half. The thunder boomed as their voice, calling out to each other. They sent down rain in response to each other's boastful claims of greatness — a hard, pounding rain that flattens crops and tears at flesh.

The rain made its way downward quickly, falling from the sky, headed for greatness. It sought out the roof of the lodge, beating it and causing the pounding sound of anger to reverberate throughout the building. It made Scott pause, hand on the door. He looked up, thinking of the foreshadowing this would have on the story he would tell later.

He attempted to turn the handle, but it wouldn't move. Of course it is locked, he thought to himself. Scott looked around, thinking of something that could help him in this situation. He studied the door again, it was large and looked solid, made of thick wooden panels. The hardware itself looked fairly old and not in the best shape. He focused on the hinges. They were large and brass — the kind with a large pin to hold them in shape. Scott pulled out his multi-tool and selected one of the attachments, holding it up to the bottom of the hinge. It looked like it would fit. He looked around, searching for something heavy.

He spied the broken leg of a small wooden cabinet that appeared to have held a vase, which had long since fallen off and had been smashed to pieces. The leg was still attached to the cabinet but at an odd angle. Scott silently made his way over to it and grabbed it, yanking. It came off easier than he expected but still took some force and whined a little bit as the nails came free. Now he found himself wielding a wooden club with nails spiking their way through to come out the other side, somewhat impressively.

He went back to the door with his newly found implement and got to work quickly, placing the multi-tool under the hinge pin and giving it a large whack, wincing at the sound it made in the hallway. It was much louder than he wanted, the pin resisting the force it took to free it. The sound emanating from the pin sounded akin to a squealing pig being forced to the slaughter. Luckily, the storm now raging outside and lashing against the roof absorbed most of the noise, covering it up.

Scott studied the pin, verifying the progress it had made. Where it had once been flush to the top of the hinge it now stuck up about a finger length. Inside, Scott felt hope but knew he had three of these to do and not a whole lot of time to do it in. He continued and banged two more times. Each time he attempted to pull the pin out, but it remained steadfast within the hinge. After one more blow he felt the pin give and rejoiced inside as it began to move when he pulled it. Quickly, he moved on to the middle pin, forcing it upward with as heavy a blow as he was willing to risk. The sound was obvious but not incredibly loud, and he thanked God that the man at the top of the stairs had been called away, otherwise he would have been discovered, and the resulting gunfire would have surely brought others.

The second pin resisted more, requiring five blows and the precious time it took to apply them, but then broke free. The last pin he left for the top hinge, giving himself the best angle and largest range of motion. He checked the hallway as he worked, stopping to listen for any sounds of someone approaching. It was still clear.

He didn't hold back on the top hinge, swinging the club with as much force as he could muster. It connected with a solid thud and

Scott felt the pin break free at once. He quickly pulled all the pins out and gripped the door from underneath. Hoping for the best he crouched down and pulled backward, nearly falling over as the door broke free from the hinges and slipped itself out of the lock. The way was now open to him, and he attempted to set the door down as silently as possible, but it still dropped against the ground with a dull thud, the weight preventing him from doing anything else. It was solid all right.

Scott stood by the entrance to the door, not knowing what could be inside. He quickly peered around the corner, attempting to determine if there were any hostiles in the room. The room looked empty, furnished with furniture that wasn't decayed and old like the other room. This one looked like someone had recently added everything, from the bed to the rugs on the floor.

It looked empty, all the chairs in the room devoid of life and no person-like silhouettes standing in the room. Had they been wrong about where he had put her? Cautiously, he entered the doorway, searching more closely.

The first thing he noticed as he entered was that the bed looked like it had been slept in and hastily remade. Then he noticed the lump under the covers. It looked body-shaped, although too small for Briana. There was another door on his left, most likely leading to a bathroom, and a bed with two chairs flanking a table in the main part of the room.

A dresser was also in the room, tucked off in the corner with a TV on it like the other room. The TV looked like it was old — no one used those anymore.

Candles adorned the horizontal sections of the furniture, haphazardly strewn around the room to give enough light to the occupant in case they needed it, and Scott could detect the faint smell of smoke, as if they had been extinguished recently and the smoke still lingered in the air.

Scott lowered his weapon, pointing the pistol at the ground as he stood in the doorway. He knew that he had made enough noise to warn anyone inside that he was coming, there was no way they would still be sleeping in the middle of a gunfight mixed with a storm and then him breaking down the door.

Slowly and silently he made his way over to the bed. He stood on the right side, over the mass and firmly grasped the edge of the covers, preparing himself for the worst. In one smooth motion he ripped the covers off the body — only to discover a mass of clothing arranged in the middle of the bed.

"What?" he said.

Suddenly, a sharp pain blossomed in his left ankle, an odd crack coming from it. Instantly, he dropped down to one leg and looked down, thinking how weird it was that a heavy metal candlestick was now protruding from underneath the bed. The pain in his ankle reminded him it was there, but from the few more moments he had to assess he didn't think it was broken.

Noise from under the bed came forth and Scott saw a figure jump up on the other side of the bed, making for the open doorway immediately. Scott's brain caught up with his eyes as he realized who the figure was.

"Briana!" he called out hesitantly, not wanting to make too much noise but wanting to stop her. The figure froze in mid-stride and turned, as if in slow motion. Their eyes connected, and Scott could see the fear and hope mixed within them.

"Scott?" she asked. He nodded. She was on him in a flash, even quicker than when she made a break for the door, embracing him and beginning to sob.

"What's going on down there?" Scott heard Rob ask in his ear. Scott was also overcome by emotion, relief mixed with joy, and Rob's voice quickly grounded him back to the situation that was reality. He pulled back from Briana's embrace and kissed her, quickly and passionately.

"I found her," Scott said. "But we have to move quickly, we're going out the window."

"No, we can't," Briana said, also quickly brought back to her senses. Scott mellowed in the sound of her voice, having replayed it in his mind many times over the past few hours. He was exhausted, and she looked just as bad. "They barred the window here. This was meant to be a prison." Scott glanced at the window and realized she was right, there was no way they were going to be exiting the lodge from this room.

"Come with me, quietly," Scott said, taking her hand and leading her to the doorway. "Rob, I'm going back to the room I entered from. I know we can get out that way."

"Roger that. I'll keep them busy for a little while longer. I'm running low on ammo," Rob replied.

"Only a little longer now, Rob," Scott said encouragingly. They reached the now-empty doorway and Scott peered around the side, checking the hallway. It was clear. They snuck out into the hallway, hugging the wall, as they heard a fresh round of gunfire burst its way through the storm. Rob was back at work. The turret had long since fallen silent, most likely disabled by the gang members somehow. A thought struck him. "Hey Rob, can you get that other turret back online? You said you only made it look like it had a malfunction, right?"

"Shoot, I completely forgot about that, good call," Rob said. Returning gunfire retorted back from the lodge side, keeping Rob pinned down. Briana and Scott continued down the hallway, keeping close to the shadows.

They approached the top of the stairs and Scott prepared his weapon, letting go of Briana's hand and grasping the pistol firmly, preparing it for use. The top of the stairs came into view, and it was empty.

Rain poured down from outside, finding cracks in the skylights above and forming a small waterfall down onto the banister and stairs. Scott motioned Briana to go ahead as he cleared both sides, keeping a lookout as she made her way across. Scott followed closely behind, moving backwards and keeping an eye on the stairs.

The noise of the storm coming into the lodge completely drowned out any chance they had of hearing footsteps. Scott found himself losing sight of the stairs as the hallway overtook it and turned back around to direct Briana to the room he had entered from. She nodded assent, and they both quickly made their way to the door.

They had just reached it when they both heard a noise. Scott turned just in time to see the man at the top of the stairs making his way into the hallway. Briana froze, and Scott pushed her quickly into the room, accidentally pushing her into the door.

He watched in horror as the door swung all the way open and crashed into the wall. Scott turned to watch the man also turn toward him. Their eyes met each other and locked on. For a few seconds no one moved.

"Hey!" the man shouted, and began to reach for his belt. He was fumbling with something on it as Scott jumped into the room.

"We better go quickly," Scott said, pulling the rope from his shoulder.

He dashed past Briana who was grabbing the door. She wrenched it shut, slamming it into the frame, and locked the deadbolt. Scott began tying the rope to the frame of the bed, still solidly holding the mass of decaying mattress.

Quickly, he tied a solid bowline and threw it over the bedpost, cinching it quickly in place and tugging. It held firmly, but he wasn't sure if it would hold both their weights so he ran to the balcony and fed it through a few balcony railings.

Briana was pulling the TV stand closer to the door, throwing the TV on the floor to crash into pieces. She wedged it against the door and dashed to help Scott. He had wound the rope around the railing a few times and was in the process of overturning the dresser when they heard the man begin to pound on the door.

"Open up in there!" he said as he pounded, jiggling the broken lock. "Aw, shit! Hey, you guys better open up in there or... or I'll shoot you!" he said. Scott set the dresser falling on the floor, conveniently wedging itself between the bed and the wall.

They were on the balcony, Scott throwing the rest of the roll of rope off, when they faintly heard the final warning above the tempest raging around them, soaking them instantly to the bone.

"This is your final warning!" the man shouted.

"OK, hold onto my back tightly," Scott told Briana. She nodded as he hooked up his auto-repelling device to the rope. The device would take some of the work off his arms, which were already pretty weak from his recent escapades.

"We're going to get out of here," he said, gazing into her eyes.

Briana saw truth deep in his eyes and trusted him, still afraid. Lightning crashed onto the roof and they both started as thunder boomed instantly, nearly knocking them off their feet. Scott felt doubt creep into his mind, wondering if he would be able to hold both of them as the storm raged around them. The cold rain drove into their clothes, stealing any warmth from them. Scott climbed over the balcony railing and assisted Briana to do the same.

She grabbed onto his back. Gunshots ripped into the door of the room, lodging themselves into the far wall behind the bed.

"Time to go," Briana said into Scott's ear hurriedly. Scott leaned back smoothly, agreeing. They felt the world lurch as Scott stopped them perpendicular to the side of the lodge.

He kicked off and heard Briana gasp as they dropped off the ledge of the balcony, dropping a few feet until Scott's feet connected with the side of the wall. Pain radiated up his left ankle, a present from Briana returning.

Scott clenched his teeth and forced the pain and exhaustion he felt deeper inside him, ignoring it for the time being, and kicked off again. Briana tracked their progress by the floor, the next kick taking them to the middle of the second floor, and then one more taking them past the window to just below the second floor.

She felt his body tense and she squeezed tighter, attempting to send her love to him as he carried them both to freedom. One more jump, lightning flashed close by. They landed and the thunder rolled over them.

They were about halfway to the ground, only a few more feet left. Gunshots continued to ring out, some from above, some from around, but blessedly nothing hit them.

One more jump and they were on the ground.

"Rob, we're out. Head to extraction," Scott said as he deftly released the auto-repeller from the rope. Briana made it to her feet as well, wiping her wet hair from her eyes and quickly tying it into a bun. "This way," Scott said to Briana, grabbing her hand and pulling her to the wall.

They crouched down and made their way to the side of the lodge, Scott scanning the area for people. They saw none and made it to the corner. Scott sneaked a peek around the corner and saw the coast was clear to the wall. He turned to look behind them.

"I've got one more present for these bastards," Rob said in his ear. Suddenly Scott and Briana heard a spinning sound and then a turret barked forth, Scott seeing the muzzle flash illuminating the roof behind him. They heard screaming coming from the other side of the lodge, and they knew that now was the time to go for it.

They both stood up and bolted, running across the open no-man's-land to the wall. The few seconds they were out in the open stretched into what seemed like minutes, both of them expecting to hear shooting break out as they broke cover and bullets to fly. Thankfully, there was none, and with each step they made closer to the wall the more hope sprang to their hearts.

Finally, they reached the tree line and Scott pulled them farther, reaching the stone wall shortly after that. They paused for a moment to catch their breaths, both looking behind them to see if they were followed. From this view they could see the other side of the lodge that had been hidden, the garage in plain view. Men were scattered around, most unmoving, with a few hidden by the wall that prevented them from being reached by either the turrets or Rob's cover fire.

"I'll have you know that this sniper rifle is really heavy," Scott heard Rob pant in his ear, clearly out of breath. The offhand comment brought light to the gruesome situation, and Scott chuckled. Briana stared at him, breathing heavily, but still able to throw a large conversation into one look, as women are apt to do. It told him how ridiculous he was for laughing in such a terrible situation and that he should really focus on the moment they were in now. Scott shook his head.

"Thanks, man," he said quietly, still chuckling a little. Scott turned back to the wall. They were safe from anyone at the moment. The hard, cold stones pressed up against his back as he leaned on it were slippery from the rain.

They were covered in moss that had soaked up the rainwater like a sponge, and he realized there were no steps in sight to be able to ascend and get over the wall. "Here," he told Briana, turning to put his back against the wall and holding his hands up so he could boost her over. She got the picture quickly and put one foot onto his hands as he squatted for maximum holding power. She grabbed as high as she could go on the wall and pushed herself up, pulling on the stones at the same time.

Briana managed to pull herself onto the wall into a laying position and quickly turned around to help Scott. He turned to face the wall and lodged his right foot into a crack in the wall, favoring his left foot that was still hurting every time he put weight on it. Grimacing, he pushed his way up, his right hand slipping off the slippery wall but his left holding. He grabbed Briana's outstretched arm and used it for support to climb up.

His left foot slipped off, nearly taking them both back off the wall, but he caught the top of the wall with his free hand and hung off. He found a better foothold and made his way onto the wall, falling into a laying position with Briana. He glanced back and was relieved to see that they were still unseen, or at least that no one was following them.

"OK, now we make it down the other side," Scott said to Briana, pulling himself into a crouching position.

"You know it's really confusing having you talk to her with me listening, right?" Rob asked. It caught Scott off guard.

"Ah, sorry, I'll try to preface my sentences next time," Scott said. Briana stared at him, clearly confused.

"Rob," he hastily added, realizing that it was confusing for her as well.

Realization filled her eyes as it clicked in her mind that he was talking to Rob over the encrypted cell-phone line. Some of the comments he had made earlier seemed to make more sense now, but there was no time to dwell on it. She grabbed Scott's hand and swung a leg out into the expanse below her, slowly lowering herself down the wall, one stone at a time, the other side not nearly as slippery. She looked down as she reached as far as their arms would go and saw she only had a few feet to go. She looked back up to Scott and let go, jumping the final few feet and landing softly on her feet.

"It isn't as slippery on this side," she called up to him. He nodded, and then pulled his head back. His feet appeared next as he swung his foot over the side of the wall, carefully climbing his way down the rocking side. He too let himself fall the last few feet as his hands left the top of the wall, and had a less graceful fall as it was a higher height to fall from. He got back up and wiped the mud off his hands onto his soaking pants and brought up his laptop, glad it was waterproof.

After pulling up a map and compass he quickly put it away and pointed to the northwest.

"This way, Briana," he said, and they both took off. It was not easy going, making their way through the overgrowth in a thunderstorm, and the lightning continued to crash around them, making them jump every time they saw it or heard thunder.

They tried to run through the forest but were slowed to a slog. It had taken Scott about ten minutes to get to the wall from the ATV the first time, but they quickly approached twenty minutes and they were still about a quarter mile away. The thunderstorm was not lessening or letting up at all, and it forced the terror in them to rise to the top. They felt the men behind them — whether they were real or not — chasing after them. Scott and Briana did not talk, continuing to be driven by fear and by the cold. Slowly, Scott could see the ATV come into view through the trees where they had tucked it back into the woods when they had arrived. Hope flooded back through Scott, knowing that it was possible they might be able to get away.

"We're at the ATV, Rob. Where are you?" Scott asked.

"I'm already here, man — just trying to get warmed up," Rob replied. Scott looked closer and saw a shape in the driver's seat. It turned to him and waved, and Scott continued to work through the underbrush with Briana, forcing themselves through the drenched forest. As they got closer Scott could tell that it was Rob, and they sped up to get out of the storm. They reached the door and Scott opened it, ushering Briana inside its warmth.

She hopped in and jumped on Rob in a huge embrace, which he heartily returned. There wasn't really room for three people in the ATV since it was designed for two, but Scott managed to push his way in and shut the door.

As soon as Briana released him from her grasp, Scott also threw Rob into a deep embrace. There were no words those first few moments of the reunion, but they spoke deeply and strongly. Relief washed through all of them, and gladness, and joy all mixed together with the remnants of adrenaline and fear mixed with pure exhaustion and spikes of pain.

Scott was never more glad to have such a great friend, and Rob was so glad they were able to save Briana. As soon as the brotherly embrace had run its course, Briana clasped onto Scott, pushing into his arms and taking his face in her hands. She caressed his face for a moment, implanting his face into her memory for as long as she would live, and then brought his face to hers in a deep, passionate kiss.

"Ooooh, you two, get a room!" Rob joked, just glad to see them both together and happy. It had been one whirlwind of a day. Their kiss lingered for a few more moments, and then they broke off, Briana content just to hug him in a tight embrace and feel enveloped by his arms. Scott grasped her tight, not wanting to let go of her ever again.

Rob started up the ATV in silent mode, not wanting to disturb them. Eventually they had their fill and released the embrace, Briana sitting between Scott and Rob, content to have his arm around her waist and rest her head on his shoulder. Scott reached forward and turned on the heater, sending luxurious heat blowing through the cab. They all sighed as it hit them, all of them realizing how wet and cold they were.

Outside, the thunderstorm was finally letting up, easing its howling wind and driving rain to a gentle shower. Holes began to appear in the cloud cover, the pre-dawn light poking its way through the large mass of black thunderheads that spewed their rain upon the world.

Rob put the ATV into manual and began heading southwest, making their way back. It was slow going through the forest, and they had just crested a hill when Rob stopped. Scott stirred, Briana asleep on his shoulder. They could see the sun rising off in the distance, its rays just peeking over the mountain range. The rain finally stopped then, the clouds beginning to disperse, colored in yellows, oranges, and reds.

Scott looked down at Briana sleeping on his shoulder, her beautiful face framed by the brilliant rays of the sun streaming in the window. He knew at that moment it had been worth it, just to save her from whatever evil awaited her. She moved and opened her eyes as the sun crested the mountain, its bright light streaming into her eyes now accustomed to the dark. His mind was made up in that moment. She looked up into his eyes, hers now adjusting to the light. Nervousness overcame him momentarily, butterflies nervously fluttering in his stomach. He pushed it to the side like he had for all the fear earlier in the night.

"Will you marry me?" he asked, no longer doubting or afraid as he used to be. She was still for a few seconds, he could see it was still sinking in. Then it hit her and she smiled.

"Yes," she said, and then he kissed her. There were no butterflies now, only certainty.

"Well, let's have a party," Rob said, and Scott glanced at him, a huge goofy smile on his face.

Eclectic Stories

Thank you for spending your precious time reading this book.

If stories make you salivate, learn more about lore, take an exclusive sneak peek behind the scenes, and get writing updates in my newsletter, Eric's Eclectic Stories.

As a bonus you'll get *Stories from the Deep*, a Patmos Sea Fantasy Adventure anthology that gives a glimpses of lore, extra prologues and epilogues, and character backstories.

If you aren't satisfied, unsubscribe at any time.

Join at erickercher.com.

-Eric Kercher

Also By Eric Kercher

Patmos Sea Fantasy Adventure Series

Fathomless Pursuit
Architect's Prize
Ironbound Path
Sunken Prey
Unanswered Prophecy
Hardened Pilgrim
Final Peace

Seventh Hall Chronicles

Seventh Hall
Ode to the Survivors
Bastion of the Deep

Epic of Hornblood Castle

Siege of the Unfinished Keep
Winter at Hornblood
Branch of the Everlong

Castlebound Adventures

Rats in the Cellar!

Anthologies

Red Eagle Anthology
Searchlight Anthology

Stand Alone

Planet Reaping
Dukedom Rumble

About Author

Eric Kercher was born and raised in a small town on the Great Plains on good books. After attending a small state school on the east coast he joined the US Navy to serve his country and explore the world. He worked on submarines, and the world beneath the waves captivated him with all its mysteries and wonders. After spending time in larger cities, he's settled down in a quiet town with his wife and children. When not on an adventure in a good book the author enjoys creating dust woodworking, architecture, and spending time with loved ones.

Find out more at www.erickercher.com.